The man was dressed in a suit, distinctly out of place here amid longhorns and chaps

He could be a businessman from Houston, but even in the city the men wore boots and Stetsons. He looked…

Cassie pulled in a sudden, shocked breath. She felt as though she'd been kicked, taken a blow, hard and fast.

Ethan.

Here. Back on Flying M property.

The man who had made her heart slip again and again into overdrive.

The man who had helped shape her entire existence.

The man who had given her Donny, the most precious thing in her life.

Dear Reader,

When I was much younger (and a lot thinner) my sister and I had horses. We spent all our free time with Shalimar, Sparky and Sheba. We rode the pine trails, played horseback hide-and-seek in the orange groves and used the rumps of our mounts as diving boards into the lake near our home. We took dozens of spills off their backs, chased them all over the pasture to get their hooves trimmed, and chanced getting nipped if we dawdled in giving them hay.

Having horses was hard work, expensive and time-consuming. But I wouldn't have missed a minute of it. They're wonderful creatures, and to this day, I still love the smell of molasses sweet feed and a leather saddle on a sweaty horse.

So I guess it's only natural that sooner or later I'd draw on all those old memories. My Texas heroine, Cassie Wheeler, has a deep love of horses, but she's seen the worst of them, too. The danger and unpredictability of a two-thousand-pound animal has left her scarred, both emotionally and physically.

Fortunately, that's where Ethan Rafferty comes in. He was in love with her before her life changed so dramatically, and he's in love with the woman she is now. Whatever the consequences, he's ready to become part of her life again. If only she'll let him.

I love to hear from readers, and a lot of romance novel fans have a love of horses, as well. Share yours by sending me an e-mail at abair@cfl.rr.com.

Happy trails!

Ann Evans

That Last Night in Texas

Ann Evans

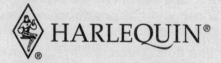

HARLEQUIN®

TORONTO • NEW YORK • LONDON
AMSTERDAM • PARIS • SYDNEY • HAMBURG
STOCKHOLM • ATHENS • TOKYO • MILAN • MADRID
PRAGUE • WARSAW • BUDAPEST • AUCKLAND

Recycling programs
for this product may
not exist in your area.

ISBN-13: 978-0-373-71660-9

THAT LAST NIGHT IN TEXAS

www.eHarlequin.com

Printed in U.S.A.

ABOUT THE AUTHOR

Ann Evans has been writing since she was a teenager, but it wasn't until she joined Romance Writers of America that she actually sent anything to a publisher. Eventually, with the help of a very good critique group, she honed her skills and won a Golden Heart from Romance Writers of America for Best Short Contemporary Romance of 1989. Since then she's happy to have found a home at Harlequin Superromance.

A native Floridian, Ann enjoys traveling, hot fudge sundaes and collecting antique postcards. She loves hearing from readers and invites them to visit her Web site at www.aboutannevans.com.

Books by Ann Evans

HARLEQUIN SUPERROMANCE

Don't miss any of our special offers. Write to us at the following address for information on our newest releases.

Harlequin Reader Service
U.S.: 3010 Walden Ave., P.O. Box 1325, Buffalo, NY 14269
Canadian: P.O. Box 609, Fort Erie, Ont. L2A 5X3

For Sherri Angell, who has never lost her passion for horses, cowboys and living life to the fullest.

CHAPTER ONE

CASSANDRA RAFFERTY. Mr. and Mrs. Ethan Rafferty. Ethan and Cassie Rafferty.

With a pleased sigh, Cassie McGuire smiled down at the delicately scrolled words she'd written in her diary. She resisted the temptation to dot the *i* in her name with a tiny heart. After all, she was two days past her eighteenth birthday and a woman now, no longer a child.

She ran her fingers over the lines, as though they were braille symbols whose importance she could discover through touch. They *were* important, because very soon this was who she would become—Cassandra Rafferty— and nothing anyone said or did could change that.

Ethan's wife.

She felt her heart go into a wild gallop. Sometimes she still couldn't believe it.

There was a knock on her bedroom door and Cassie jumped, startled. As usual, her father didn't wait for permission to enter. She had little time to slip her diary into her desk drawer before he appeared.

"It's getting late, cupcake," Mac McGuire said, offering her a tentative smile. They had barely escaped an argument earlier this evening, and he was obviously hoping all was forgiven.

She couldn't leave tonight without trying to make it

right between them. Crossing the room, she gave him a hug.

He was a big man, barrel-chested, with skin turned to leather by years of riding in the hot sun. His full name was Donald Alastair McGuire, Scottish through and through, but everyone in East Texas called him Mac. The Flying M wasn't the biggest ranch in the Beaumont area, and it certainly wasn't the richest, but her father was well-liked and respected.

Cassie adored him. After her mother's death, it had been just the two of them. He was a good, loving father, a man of strong opinions, but possessing a tender heart. Especially where she was concerned.

Unfortunately, he could also be unbearably overprotective, and she hated that her marriage to Ethan had had to be planned in secret. When their absence was discovered tomorrow, her dad would be hurt and angry. Better to face him afterward with marriage license in hand. He would come to terms with it, though she couldn't bear the idea that he might not. But somehow, one day, she would make it up to him.

"I'm heading over to the Wheeler place for a little while," he said.

"Now? It's so late."

Josh Wheeler lived at the next ranch over from the Flying M. He had inherited River Bottom after his parents were killed in a car accident last year. The place was small, but had great potential, and Cassie's father seemed to have taken Josh under his wing.

"Josh says his prize mare is looking colicky. Probably nothing, but I thought I'd drive over and take a peek. I suspect he's just lonely and wanting company on a Saturday night."

Oh, no, you don't, Cassie thought. *You're not drawing me back into a discussion about how I ought to spend more time with him*. Josh Wheeler was twenty-five. He was smart, had sunny good looks and had been her best friend for years. Lately, he'd made it pretty clear that he had a romantic interest in her as well.

Unfortunately, she felt nothing for him except friendship.

In fact, tonight's near argument had been over Josh, who had asked her out on a date. She'd refused. Her father had thought she ought to reconsider, and Cassie had been forced to dig in and defend her decision without revealing the basic truth of the situation.

How could she go on a date with one man, when in less than twenty-four hours, she'd be married to another?

A sudden niggling worry made Cassie bite the inside of her cheek. In a few hours she was supposed to meet Ethan in the horse barn. The last thing she needed was to run into her father coming in the front door as she was going out. She'd have to be extra careful.

She faked a yawn. "Well, have fun, but don't stay out too late. Since tomorrow's Sunday, I think I'll sleep in."

"Don't forget that we're going to work Bandera at ten. Time for me to see what I've gotten myself into."

Bandera was the new chestnut stallion her father had purchased during his last trip to Dallas. He'd been delivered today, and from the glimpse Cassie had seen of him from her bedroom window, his sleek red coat and her father's auburn hair would make an arresting, impressive sight.

"Is Ethan supposed to help?" Cassie couldn't resist asking.

Her father shook his head. "The horse doesn't need to be broken. He just needs some manners."

"You will be careful, won't you? You're too old to be getting bounced."

"Brat! Not too old to keep young stallions and impudent daughters in line," he said, reaching out to tweak her nose. "I know how to keep my mind in the middle. But don't worry, I told Ethan to make sure Bandera stays tranked until we give him a workout tomorrow. Just a small second dose to keep him calm. I don't want all that pent-up energy exploding under me before I get a read on him." Her dad gave her an odd look. "Why do you ask if Ethan's involved?"

"Just curious," Cassie said with deliberate nonchalance. Had she been foolish to mention Ethan's name? "I like watching him work the horses."

"Stay away from him. He could use some manners, too."

"I don't—"

"I mean it. He's too rough around the edges to associate with anyone but the crew."

"Dad!"

Cassie couldn't help that surprised response. Her father never spoke about anyone this way. She tried not to look defensive or hurt, but the remark worried her a little. Once she was married, it would be crucial that the two men she loved most in the world get along.

"He seems very nice to me," she said quietly.

"I didn't say he wasn't nice, although he seems to like horses better than people. I said he was rough around the edges. He's good at what he does and he learns quickly.

He could make something of himself one day when he's ready to settle down, but that's a long way off. Stick to men like Josh."

Predictable men like Josh, she amended in her head.

To cut the conversation short, Cassie produced another yawn and caught the edge of her door. "I'll see you in the morning," she said.

He chucked her on the chin and started to turn away.

"Dad." Impulsively, she caught his arm, and when he turned back, she looked him directly in the eyes. Her senses were dull with misery at the realization that, after tonight, nothing between them would ever be quite the same. "You do know I love you, don't you?"

He grinned. "Love you, too, cupcake. More than life itself."

She rose up on tiptoes to kiss his cheek. Her throat suddenly felt tight at the thought of leaving him, deceiving him. But what else could she do?

Her decision had been made. She'd finally gotten up the nerve to follow her heart, and she wouldn't change her mind.

Not even for a father she loved dearly.

PRECISELY AT MIDNIGHT, Cassie slipped down the stairs, suitcase in hand. She didn't think her father had returned from the Wheeler place yet. The ranch truck wasn't parked out front, and there was definitely no snoring coming from his room.

Careful, Cassie. The first real adventure of your life. Don't blow it now.

She quietly let herself out and hurried along the path

to the horse barn. Her heart was pounding in her chest. Not from fear, really, although it would be horrible if she was caught; mostly it was excitement that left her breathless with anticipation. In a matter of hours she and Ethan would be married, starting a brand-new life together. The night felt as though it held magic.

When they'd first met a year ago, he'd seemed so foreign, so different from the usual men who came looking for work at the ranch. He had shown up to apply for one of the wrangler jobs, without a horse, a dog for company or even a well-worn duffel bag. He didn't look or act like the other hands on the Flying M. The crews who worked the herds were either grizzled older men with a lifetime of scars and tall tales behind them, or college kids playing cowboy until school started again.

Ethan seemed to be neither. At twenty-one, he already had the physique of a man, with the soft edges of boyhood filed down to toned, lean muscle. He was handsome, but in a rough, slightly battered kind of way that actually made him seem better-looking than if he'd been conventionally attractive. And that devilish twist to his mouth—that made him seem slightly dangerous.

She'd heard that he didn't smoke or drink, and he kept to himself, never joining the other men who went into town on Saturday nights. Her father said he took his job seriously, which was a good thing, because everyone knew Mac McGuire didn't put up with slackers on the Flying M.

Initially, when their paths crossed, Ethan had been respectful of her position as the owner's only child, but he still unnerved her. He seemed so self-contained, almost secretive. Sometimes she had caught him watching her—a glimpse of soulful blue eyes under those long, dark lashes that perfectly matched his silky-looking black hair. She'd pretended to ignore his surveillance, but inside she had shivered.

He still made her shiver—though for completely different reasons now.

The barn door creaked open on rusted hinges. Several of the horses along the corridor moved restively and stuck their heads out of their stalls. Midnight visitors were uncommon at the Flying M.

She found Ethan in the tack room, and slipped up behind him to place her hands over his eyes. "Guess who? And if you say any name but mine, the wedding's off."

He turned and grabbed her up, grinning. "Hey there, darlin'. What's your name again?"

She laughed softly and punched his arm. He responded by giving her the kind of kiss she'd never experienced from anyone but him. He smelled of leather and spice and a heated male energy that sent tingles through her stomach.

She bathed in the heady delight of his touch, his scent, the nudge of his thighs against her legs. Her body hummed and sizzled, sparked by nothing more than simple contact, and he knew it instantly because he kissed her again, more slowly, more thoroughly this time.

She nestled against him, and when his hands pushed under her thin blouse, cupping her breasts, she almost stopped breathing. He was coaxing her body to life, his eyes speaking volumes of need and want and desire, and Cassie couldn't help but answer.

Slowly, savoring every murmur and sigh, she let her head fall back. She clutched his dark hair in both hands, bringing his head down. Ethan's mouth came against the pulse point at her throat, stroking with his tongue, teasing, raking his teeth lightly against her skin until she felt consumed by fire.

She let her fingers trail along his strong back, thinking of all the ways she'd daringly slide her hand down his body the next time they made love. They'd been intimate twice before, but she had been embarrassingly unskilled and nervous. Tomorrow, she would find the courage to be the aggressor.

She adored the weight and shape of him, the coiled strength of his biceps and the taut muscles of his stomach. His fingers were callused, and their texture as they moved over her body made a quick, jittery thrill trip through her.

She wanted more. She wished desperately for it.

But when Ethan's hand slipped to the top button of Cassie's jeans, her hand stopped him. She straightened as best she could, and though her body protested the separation, her brain demanded they go no further.

"We can't," she whispered against his ear. "We have to leave."

"You're early."

"I'm *on time*," she said as she shifted her clothes back into order.

"I hate a clock watcher."

"You should have thought of that before you proposed." Ethan's one failing—at least the only one she'd found so far—was that he was seldom punctual for anything unless it was a direct order from her father. "Still want to marry me?" she asked, smiling up at him and trailing a finger across his bottom lip.

He growled low and brushed his stubbled chin gently

against her cheeks, as though branding her. "Yes, I want to marry you. I want to make love to you. I want to make babies with you and watch them grow up to make babies of their own." He caught her face in his hands so that their eyes met. "Good enough for you, princess?"

"Yes." She exhaled with a happy sigh. She loved this about him—the secret, tender sincerity beneath the rough, sexy exterior that everyone else saw. She liked to think that she was the only one who knew the real Ethan Rafferty, though the truth was, she'd fallen so quickly, so hopelessly in love that she knew little more about him than the most basic facts.

He talked so seldom about his past. She knew only that he'd walked away from an abusive home when he was eighteen and that his father had been a horse trainer in Kentucky, a great one, but that talent had drowned in buckets of booze.

For three years Ethan had drifted, but the talent with horses that he'd inherited from his father had made him believe he had a future. Someday.

Just who was this man she intended to marry? Was she really willing to walk out of the pampered life she had known, cut herself loose from her youth and the adoring shelter of her father's love to set her future on this unknown path?

Yes, she thought. It didn't matter. She knew enough. She knew the essentials of Ethan Rafferty, the shape of his courage, the depth of his heart, that quiet confidence that could make her believe that anything was possible. And it pleased her to think that she'd have an eternity to find out everything else about him.

He had latched on to one of her long, red curls, rubbing it between his fingers as though testing it somehow.

He loved playing with her hair. She pulled the lock through his fingers. "Stop that. I want it to look halfway decent tonight."

His fingers cupped her face. "*Decent* is much too ordinary a word to describe what I see when I look at you."

She lowered her head, embarrassed by the way his eyes caressed her.

A slow smile twisted his lips. "You really have no idea how beautiful you are, do you?"

She had no illusions about her looks. She might be blessed with her father's dark red hair, but she could never do anything with it thanks to the humidity of East Texas. She had inherited her mother's ready smile, but her lips lacked that full, pouty look that seemed to make men drool. For a while Cassie had actually prayed to have a perky cheerleader's nose, but with her Scottish heritage there was little chance of that.

As for the spunky personality she'd longed for to offset her mundane features, it had never developed. The truth was, most of the time she was shy, contemplative and given to playing it safe. Only Ethan seemed to bring out her wilder side, her adventurous spirit. She knew her weaknesses. That he seemed to find her remarkable in any way both delighted and surprised her.

Feeling awkward, she gave him one last kiss and stepped back, suddenly all business. "Enough flattery. You've already won me over. Dad's at Josh's place, but I don't know how much longer he'll be there. We need to get on the road."

"We should just wait for him," Ethan said. "Tell him we're getting married, and we hope we'll have his blessing, but—"

"Are you insane?" Cassie exclaimed. "We can't do that."

He tilted his head as though examining her closely. "Why?"

"Because he'd never give his blessing."

"Because you're too young to get married? Or because you want to marry *me?*"

"Trust me. I know Dad." She stroked her hand along his arm, hoping to ease the slight trace of hurt she thought she saw in his eyes. "Please, Ethan. Let's just go."

He grimaced, then nodded. "I'm almost ready. I'm just leaving a note for Hank to check Cisco in the morning. I think he's coming down with thrush again, and I want to suggest a new treatment." When she gave him a look, he waved his hand dismissively. "I'll only be a minute. Go check out your dad's new toy. He's a beauty, and he'll probably be glad to see a friendly face. Last stall on the left."

Her body still humming with the residue of passion, Cassie took the suggestion and wandered down the barn's dimly lit corridor. No point hanging over Ethan like a puppy. Besides, she was curious about Bandera.

The end stall was slightly larger than the rest, but the chestnut stallion within made it seem small. Bandera was tall for a quarter horse, at least sixteen hands, with deep, muscular shoulders and the powerful hindquarters so common to the breed. In the diminished light he looked almost bloodred.

He was magnificent, and Cassie regretted that she wouldn't be here to see her father's first real contact with the animal. They were definitely going to make a striking pair.

The hayrack overhead was nearly empty. Bandera nibbled halfheartedly at the remaining flake of Bermuda grass, but pawed the floorboards as though annoyed there wasn't more.

"You've got quite an appetite, don't you, fella?" she said, holding out her hand.

Bandera's ears pricked forward, and he turned in Cassie's direction to rub his face against her palm. She wished she had some treat to give him.

To make up for the fact that she didn't, she spent a minute or two stroking his head and raking her fingernails gently under his chin. He was calm and well-mannered, very sweet really, for a stallion. The big horse blew out a contented snort. Evidently the second tranquilizer Ethan had given Bandera had the animal under tight control.

"You're just a big baby," she whispered to him. "Don't worry. You're going to like it here."

The stallion turned away to pull the last of the hay out of the rack. Cassie glanced down the aisleway. Still no Ethan.

Spotting a pitchfork nearby, she retrieved it and speared a fresh flake of Bermuda grass. Might as well make herself useful while she waited.

She swung the hay up and over the stall wall, hoping it would drop squarely into the rack. It didn't. Instead, it landed on the stall's floor and broke apart.

Damn. As a kid, her baling arm had been pretty good, but she supposed it had been too long since she'd had to use it. Bandera would trample the sweet-smelling strands to dirty straw in no time, and the stallion shouldn't eat compromised hay.

Wishing Ethan would hurry, Cassie pulled the latch

on the half door and entered the stall. Bandera's ears pricked forward in attention, and he eyed her curiously. She nudged the animal aside with her shoulder so she could reach the hay to repitch it.

This time her aim was better. It went right into the rack, and immediately the horse stretched his neck to pull down a mouthful.

"How's that?" Cassie asked as she stroked his powerful neck and crooned soft words. She had her father's love for horses. Standing this close, Bandera was even more beautiful. A coat like warm silk. Proud head and sleek lines. She'd bet he'd have the gait of a rocking horse.

"Cassie, get out of there!"

A male voice behind her made Cassie and Bandera both jump. Ethan was at the stall's entrance, already sliding back the latch. He looked surprised and angry, as though she had no right to be inside.

She made a face at him as she entwined her fingers around the stallion's halter. "Ease up, cowboy. We're just getting acquainted."

"Come out. *Now.*"

Bandera jerked his head, clearly disliking the sound of harsh voices. Cassie wasn't all that thrilled herself. Ethan's attitude annoyed her; the stallion was as much her horse as her father's, and Ethan had no right to order her around.

She tossed her hair over one shoulder, intent on telling him what he could do with his demands. He wasn't her husband *yet,* she would teasingly inform him. "I'm just—"

With her hand still on Bandera's halter, the horse nearly pulled her arm out of its socket as he jerked his head again. With flattened ears and rolling eyes, the stallion suddenly came to life.

Cassie's hold was ripped loose as Bandera swung away. Ethan rushed forward to calm the animal, and just as quickly the horse lowered his head and struck out with one back leg, whacking Cassie on the left knee. The pain was immediate, intense. Somehow she kept from going down completely, knowing that to do so would mean the end of her if Bandera couldn't be quieted.

Everything seemed to happen so fast. She heard the stallion's harsh whinny and the click of teeth as he tried to bite Ethan. She stumbled toward the stall door, but the horse was everywhere—a kicking, rearing red demon that couldn't be avoided.

She saw Ethan's hand—strangely bloody—flashing out to yank her to safety, but Bandera backed into her and dragged their stretching fingers apart. As the horse reared, his hooves slipped out from under him on the bare boards. Cassie looked up to see Bandera's back coming toward her as the animal screamed in fear. She tried to move, but there was nowhere to go, and she found herself being carried down, down. Suddenly she lay crushed against the straw with the panicked horse thrashing on top of her.

Ethan was shouting, calling her name, but she couldn't speak. The air had left her lungs. She didn't know what happened after that. Maybe she blacked out. When she opened her eyes again, she was still on the floor, but Bandera was gone.

She blinked up to find Ethan hovering over her.

"Be still." His voice sounded shaky and more uncertain than she'd ever heard it. He brushed her long hair out of her eyes. "I'm going for help."

Too shocked to do more than nod, Cassie was barely aware of his quick kiss. Then he was gone.

As though from far away, she heard one desperate whinny. She tried to concentrate on taking deep breaths, but every pull of air felt like shards of glass in her lungs. The pain was suddenly unbearable, as if someone had set fire to her chest, hip and left leg. Was she going to die right here? Right now?

How could she? Today was her wedding day.

She stared at the bare boards of the barn's roof, waiting for Ethan to return. Her mind drifted as she lay still. Perfectly, utterly still. Somewhere in that awful silence the truth came to her, spinning away in a mist of pain and fear.

Mrs. Ethan Rafferty. Cassandra Rafferty.

Such a lovely, lovely dream…

But not tonight.

CHAPTER TWO

ETHAN SAT SLUMPED in an emergency room chair, watching blood pool slowly into the cupped palm of his left hand.

Under the ripped mess that had once been his favorite jacket, his biceps burned. He was pretty sure that if he could find the strength to peel off the bloodstained material, he would see a sizable bite mark where Bandera's teeth had caught him. As it was, he knew his arm was broken.

God, what was Cassie doing, going into that stall? And why didn't I think to tell her that Bandera wasn't sedated?

His hand fisted around the blood. His muscles turned to fire with that movement, but Ethan almost welcomed the pain. He didn't care if his damned arm fell off. The only thing that mattered right now was Cassie, who'd disappeared into the chaos and mystery of one of the hospital's trauma rooms. She'd been so pale, barely conscious, as though her life was slipping away like a frightened ghost.

Ethan ducked his head, praying for the first time in years. His mother had dragged him to church when he was a kid, but after her death, his father, who had no use for God or anyone else, had never made him go back.

Please, God. Not Cassie. Anything you want from me. Just not Cassie.

The doors from the ambulance bay slid open with a whoosh, and Ethan looked up to see Mac McGuire and Josh Wheeler hurrying toward him. McGuire's lips were tight with anger, his eyes wild and searching.

It occurred to Ethan that very soon Cassie's father would hate him. And tonight, he thought, the man had good reason to.

Ethan rose, waiting. The room started to spin, but he gritted his teeth and refused to give in to it.

"What happened?" McGuire demanded.

"Cassie went into Bandera's stall. The animal spooked. He reared and went over on top of her."

"Dear God," Josh muttered.

McGuire frowned. "How is that possible? The horse was tranked. He should have been asleep on his feet."

"He wasn't because I…" Ethan lifted his chin. He knew a confession would be the end of the joy he'd found at the Flying M, but he had no choice. "I—I don't like tranquilizing horses, and I didn't think he needed the second one."

"*You* didn't think!" McGuire bellowed. A couple of people in the waiting room glanced at him nervously. "Since when do you know more about horses than I do? And you let Cassandra go into that stall, when I expressly told you that no one was to go near Bandera tonight?"

"Mr. McGuire," Ethan began, "I'm sorry—"

"You don't know how sorry you'll be if anything happens to my baby."

At eighteen, Cassie was hardly a baby. She'd been

sheltered by this man all her life, but now wasn't the time to argue about how overprotective he was.

"You're fired," her father continued. "Get your stuff and get off my ranch tonight, before I kill you with my bare hands."

The older man actually took a step forward. Frankly, Ethan wouldn't have cared if he got the beating of his life. He figured it was no more than he deserved.

As though trying to deflect McGuire, Josh Wheeler slid between them. "What does the doctor say? Maybe we should try to get some answers."

McGuire nodded vaguely, obviously trying to bring himself back from the brink of violence. He turned away, and almost on some sort of stage cue, one of the emergency room doctors appeared through the double doors. He looked so grim that the bottom dropped out of Ethan's stomach.

"Cassandra McGuire's family?" the physician called to the roomful of minor burns, broken bones and shell-shocked bystanders.

Mac McGuire crossed the distance between them, and Wheeler followed. Despite the fact that the older man would not want him there, Ethan moved forward as well.

McGuire introduced himself, and the doctor wasted no time getting to the point. "She's stabilizing, and we're taking her to surgery in a few minutes. She's bleeding internally and she has some broken ribs, a collapsed lung and possibly a ruptured spleen. It's serious, but I believe we can get her through it. However…"

McGuire's face was no more than a crumpled mass of wrinkles. He looked stunned, and something in the doctor's face sent another chill down Ethan's spine.

"What else?" he asked.

The doctor gave Cassie's father a grave look. "Her left leg took quite a beating. It's fractured in three places, and the foot's badly mangled. We have an excellent orthopedic surgeon here, but I think you should be prepared for the worst."

"What's the worst?"

"Amputation of the limb."

The blood sang in Ethan's head, and all that was left of his heart, wrapped inside a miserable bundle of flesh, nearly stuttered to a halt. He was dimly aware of Cassie's father talking to the doctor, but he had to blink a couple of times before he could focus. His beautiful Cassie. Less than two hours ago he'd held her against his body, and she had seemed so lush, so full of vibrant life. This couldn't be happening. It couldn't...

Oh, God, don't... Don't...

"Does she know?" McGuire asked.

"Yes. We needed her permission if the leg can't be saved."

"You should have come to me."

"Mr. McGuire, legally your daughter's an adult."

Ethan wasn't interested in this conversation. He caught the doctor's attention. "Can I see her?"

The man glanced uncertainly from Ethan back to McGuire. "She's been given something for the pain, so she's pretty well out of it. But family members can go in for a few moments before we take her up."

When Ethan started to follow in the doctor's wake, Cassie's father grabbed his uninjured arm. The look in his eyes was steely. "I thought I told you to get out of here."

Ethan stood as tall as his battered body would allow.

He supposed it was now or never. "I'm not going anywhere. I love her, Mr. McGuire."

There was a brief throb of silence.

"*Love* her?" her father finally said in a surprised, low voice. He moved threateningly close. "What are you talking about?"

"Cassie and I have been in love for several months. It's not important right now to explain how it happened, it just did."

McGuire shook his head. He looked like a bull that had just rammed a concrete post. "If you love my daughter, you'll leave her alone. You're not good for her, and if you ever needed proof of that, this is it."

"Cassie's not a child, sir. You can't control her life."

The man's face went a shade darker, if that was even possible. Wheeler moved nervously. "How dare you?" McGuire snapped. "Do you think I don't know what you want? There isn't anyone in the state who doesn't know Cassie gets everything when I die."

Ethan felt his body go tense and tight. "You think I want her money? You don't—"

"I think you're a badass, amoral drifter without a dime to his name who thinks he's found a golden goose. I think you're the worst thing in the world for my daughter. She doesn't need you. She needs stability, nurturing, someone with good judgment. She's fragile."

In spite of everything, Ethan almost laughed out loud. Cassie—fragile? Her father didn't have a clue how completely untrue that claim was. She might be quiet, even shy with others, but with him... What would her old man say if Ethan told him how her eyes could flash like blue fire in candlelight? How deep and throaty her voice could sound in the throes of passion?

He felt a weariness that was almost too much to bear. He couldn't tell McGuire any of that. Love was one thing, but seduction? Impossible for the man to digest and accept right now. What he managed to say instead was, "You want the Flying M to be a pretty prison for her, don't you?"

"Better a prison than a cemetery plot," McGuire said. He looked suddenly undone, his eyes clouded with tears. "I pray it's not too late to keep that from happening."

He swung around and stalked through the double doors, leaving Ethan weaving on his feet next to Josh.

The young rancher guided him to a nearby chair. "You've done enough damage for now. Sit down." He blew air through his lips. "Damn. I've never seen him this mad."

"He's just afraid for Cassie."

"Yeah, but he's gonna have your ass on a plate if you don't watch out." Josh angled a look toward Ethan. "You're really in love with her?"

"Hopelessly."

"She never told me. I thought we might—hell, right now it doesn't matter what I thought, does it?"

Wheeler left him then. Ethan didn't know how long he sat there, watching the doors that led to patient trauma rooms. He wasn't going anywhere until he saw Cassie himself, but he couldn't seem to find the energy to move.

He was furious with McGuire and scared for Cassie, but his mind wouldn't let go of one insistent question. Cassie wasn't the delicate flower her father thought she was, but *was* Ethan the right man for her?

It was strange how quickly they had forged a bond once they got past her initial reserve and his belief that she was nothing more than a snotty, privileged Daddy's girl. Yes, they came from different worlds, but they had some of the same dreams and similar ideas, whispered in the dark as their relationship blossomed into a physical one. And none of it had anything to do with what Cassie would inherit from her father.

If anything happens to her...

Josh Wheeler was suddenly standing over him. "You hanging in?"

Ethan nodded, though just barely.

"Cassandra's being taken to surgery soon. Mac has gone to Admitting." Josh bent to give Ethan a meaning-ful look. "I ought to have my head examined, but...I'll keep him there as long as I can if you have any plans. I just don't want to know what they are."

With his good hand, Ethan squeezed Josh's shoulder as he stood. "Thanks, man. I owe you."

He walked with slow deliberation toward the swinging doors that led to patient trauma rooms. The place was busy enough that it was possible nobody would notice one more person rushing past. Before he'd become such a loser, his father had always told him, "Act like you belong, and people will assume that you do."

No one stopped him. He went down a long corridor where most of the rooms were occupied. He heard the hiss of equipment, the low moans of someone in pain, and in one room, a cluster of people were weeping softly behind a curtain.

None of that prepared him for the sight of Cassie. The small room was a mess, cluttered with equipment and its floor littered with bloody bandages. A small pile of rags lay in one corner, and Ethan realized it was her blouse and jeans, obviously cut into pieces to remove them. As for Cassie, she was in the center of all this, on a stretcher, as white as the sheet that covered her.

He pulled the privacy curtain in place and stepped forward until he could touch her face. His skull was pounding so hard it felt made of glass.

"Cass," he whispered. "Cassie."

Her eyes were closed, but they fluttered open when he spoke her name. Her brow puckered. Her eyes were blank for a moment and he felt like dying, but then she finally focused. "Ethan…?" The word came out on a raspy whisper.

"I'm here. It's going to be all right. You'll see. I love you so much."

"Such…a stupid…mistake."

"I know." He laid the back of his hand against her cheek, which was scraped raw. He wanted so badly to ease her anguish, but he didn't know how. "I'm so sorry. Will you ever forgive me?"

"No." She turned her head slightly away from his fingers. "Don't…don't touch."

"It will be all right," he said again quickly, thinking that he'd somehow caused her more pain. "You're going to come through this just fine, and when you're all better, we can make new plans." He bent to place his mouth against her ear. "You and me—we have a date with the justice of the peace, remember?"

"I want…"

"What do you want, sweetheart?" he asked, brushing hair away from her forehead. "Some water? A nurse?"

"I want…" She stopped to lick her lips. Her gaze swung back to him, and again she seemed to be trying hard to concentrate. "I want you…to leave me alone. I don't want to…marry…you."

It felt suddenly as though someone had opened a door in his heart and let in the north wind. He shook his head. It had to be the medication talking. It *had* to be. "You don't mean that."

"I do," she said more strongly, then winced. "Just… go away."

"Cassie… Just think about getting better right now. We can talk later."

Her head rolled back and forth. "No…no…" With obvious effort, she looked him directly in the eyes. Every breath seemed to be a struggle. "We're too…too different. We have to accept…you'll never…fit in my world… and I don't…don't want yours." She sighed heavily and closed her eyes. "I mean it. I don't want…to see you anymore."

"Cass—"

"Please…" she moaned. Tears leaked out from under her lids and slid down each side of her face. "Please… go away! It's…over."

Stunned, Ethan just stared at her, not knowing what to do. This couldn't be happening. She was afraid. Confused. Drugged out of her mind. Or maybe her father had gotten to her. Whatever the truth was, he wouldn't argue with her now. She was too weak and in pain.

A nurse entered and came up beside him. "You shouldn't be in here."

Numbly, he left the room.

His mouth was dry with panic. The grimmest sense of hopelessness overtook him. Could Cassie really mean what she'd said?

He could understand why she would hate him. What he had done was unforgivable. But did she really think he wasn't good enough for her?

Back in the waiting room, he simply folded up and landed in one of the chairs because his knees were shaking so badly. He hunched forward, his arm throbbing all the way to his shoulder.

His vision grew hazy, and a sudden thickness lodged in his throat. He hadn't cried since the day they'd buried his mother, and he'd sworn never to break down again, but he couldn't seem to help it now. He felt as if he were imploding, and he didn't know what to do about it.

Someone dropped into the chair beside him. It was Josh Wheeler.

"Man, what a night," the man said with an exhausted-sounding sigh. He frowned at Ethan. "You okay?"

Ethan wiped his hand over his face, trying to compose himself. "No."

"McGuire's following Cassandra up to surgery, then camping out in the waiting room until it's over. My advice is not to be around him right now. Not unless you want to go for round two with the guy and maybe end up in jail."

Ethan barely registered those words. He stared straight ahead, thinking.

"Listen, if I were you, I'd get out of here. Mac's talking about having you arrested. Reckless endangerment, and whatever else they'll let him come up with. He's damned mad, Ethan. What the hell were you thinking, putting the moves on the boss's daughter?"

"I was thinking that I loved her. I was thinking I was good enough…" He left the rest unfinished because his voice had dried up, died, in the back of his throat.

Josh shook his head. "I'm sorry. Let's just pray that she pulls through." He stood. "I'm heading upstairs." Giving him the once-over, Josh added, "You had anybody take a look at you yet?"

"No."

He swore under his breath. "What do they expect you to do, set your own arm? I'll stop at the desk and demand some help. In spite of you being a complete lunkhead, I suppose you're still worth saving."

Ethan watched Josh walk away. The waiting room was more crowded now, filled with the fallout from another wild Saturday night. He didn't know how long he sat there, feeling as if he was in a corner from which he could not escape. His mind was just one terrible blank, except for that same litany that went round and round in his head and wouldn't let go.

Was he worth saving? Was he worth anything at all?

For years he had tried to distance himself from his upbringing. He'd left home at eighteen, scared but determined to make a better life. In the past three years he'd started to feel the difference—the respect and confidence his expertise with horses had brought him. The sense that one day he could actually be someone.

But here, right now, he was still a nobody who had come from nothing. If they married, what kind of life could he give Cassie? Her father would probably disown her. There was no way McGuire would accept him as a son-in-law now and welcome him back on the Flying M. Take him under his wing.

Ethan had plans for the future and a little money saved. But not much. No home. No car. They'd be like gypsies, going from place to place. It would be a disaster. Cassie was right. That kind of helter-skelter life was too different from what she was used to. He wouldn't be marrying her, he'd be *sentencing* her.

It couldn't work between them, and no matter how much it hurt his pride and stung to hear it, he knew it was true. And in that moment he knew what he had to do.

His blood pumped through his veins like wildfire, but he managed to stand. Though his legs threatened to buckle, somehow he put one foot in front of the other and made his way toward the sliding double doors that led out of the hospital.

Outside it was raining, hard, and in spite of the streetlights and neon entrance sign, the darkness seemed so black it had no dimension. Although he had no idea yet just where he was going, Ethan lowered his head against the pelting downpour and hurried along the sidewalk.

His teeth clenched in despair as the blood ran in rivulets under his jacket and down his hand. It splashed onto the pavement, a bright, ruby-red pattern that was washed away in moments.

CHAPTER THREE

Thirteen years later

"WELL? WHAT DO YA THINK?" Meredith Summerlin asked. "Isn't it as pretty as a Texas bluebonnet?"

Ethan looked at the Realtor he'd hired over the phone last week. She was sharp and ambitious, but she obviously saw herself as Annie Oakley reincarnated.

A passably attractive blonde with model-white teeth and a perky smile, the woman dressed as though she'd just come off a Western movie set. Fringed jacket, cowgirl hat and boots. Buxom as an overstuffed turkey. Only the fact that she carried a clipboard instead of a six-shooter killed the fantasy.

They had walked some of the property, and now they leaned against Meredith's SUV in the pleasant April sunshine. The broad field in front of them could have been the middle of nowhere, but the Texas land was just what Ethan wanted—gently rolling meadows of grass, an occasional stand of oak trees for shade, and easy frontage to the highway that led back to Beaumont.

"I like it," he agreed, and Meredith's smile got wider as she envisioned a potential sale.

"So you think it would work for what you have in mind?" she asked, inspecting him like a cop.

"Possibly."

Actually, it was *perfect* for what he had in mind, something he had known from the moment Meredith had told him yesterday that the property was on the market. After all, thirteen years ago he'd ridden this ground dozens of times.

It was part of the Flying M Ranch.

Meredith retrieved two bottles of water from a cooler in the backseat of her car and passed one to Ethan. "If you don't mind my asking, what use *would* you make of it?" She squinted down at his business card, caught by its corner on her clipboard. "What exactly is Horse Sense? You break horses?"

She sounded skeptical, and he wasn't surprised. Dressed in an expensive suit, and a silk shirt, and without the requisite Texas Stetson and boots, he didn't look like a wrangler. Knowing that he was coming back here after all these years, he hadn't intended to.

"Not anymore," Ethan admitted, taking a sip of the cold water. "Until recently, I've taught difficult horses and their owners to overcome their fears. A spooked horse is a danger to everyone around it, and I offer a behavioral clinic that builds confidence in the rider and acclimates the animal to the triggers that make it want to buck or rear."

"So you're looking to branch out?"

"In a way," Ethan said. "I'll need about two hundred acres."

He surveyed the land that would become a big part of his future—whether a failure or a success. Two months ago he'd contracted with the Mounted Police Association to develop a program exclusively for them. Instead of a weekend course, it would be a six-week one. Complete with obstacle courses, barns to stable the mounts and a few simple log cabins the men could share.

Meredith glanced at her MLS sheet on the property. "Just about the right size, I'd say. And it's been on the market for a few months."

"As I mentioned to you on the phone, I'd like to put this sale on the fast track. Financing is already lined up. It will be a cash deal."

The woman looked practically giddy with excitement. "Wonderful! Financing and the land survey are really the only holdup these days, and the property was surveyed last year. The title company should have no problem with providing a clean deed. I'd say this can be a done deal in less than two weeks."

"Perfect. That would leave me almost two months to have the place up and running by the middle of June."

"I'm sure it won't be a problem. You've done so much of the preliminary work already, you barely even need me!" Meredith frowned, aware that, for the sake of her commission, she should have left off that last statement. She recovered quickly, smiling up at Ethan. "Why don't we see if I can get a little negotiating room in the price?"

"You know the owner?" he asked, canceling the impulse to admit that he already knew this was McGuire land.

"I've lived in Beaumont for only a couple of years, so I can't say we're tight, but everyone knows the Flying M. Shall we go talk to the seller?"

They got back into the car. Meredith left the area in a swirl of dust as the vehicle bounced onto the dirt road. Ethan remembered that, from here, the Flying M was no more than a three-minute ride.

He wanted to see what information he could get from Meredith about the McGuires, but before he could lead her into answering questions she went off on problems she was experiencing with her own horse, a pinto named Goody that wouldn't walk through standing water.

Ethan nodded and listened with half an ear. He tried to convince himself that he was calm inside, but there was no denying his heart was racing about as fast as a Thoroughbred coming down the homestretch.

Thirteen years since he'd left this place, and only once had he ever come back. He'd changed so much since that frantic, frightening night in Beaumont's E.R. Sometimes the year he'd worked on the Flying M seemed like a blur, a dream.

Especially when he thought about Cassie.

He had walked out of the hospital and out of her world, broken and bloodied, but determined not to be defeated. At first, bad luck had dogged his heels like a faithful hound, and everything he'd touched had turned to shit. He hadn't much cared. A hollow feeling had lain inside him, as though someone had scooped out his vital organs. He'd thought he would be part of Cassie's future, and the next thing he knew, he'd been drop-kicked into her past.

There was no denying that a part of him had embraced bitterness and an irrational desire to prove himself. Leaving Cassie and the Flying M behind, he was back at square one, which meant doing whatever it took to survive.

He soon realized that the most dangerous, least desirable work often paid the most. Hazardous jobs in remote, unpleasant places became his bread and butter.

Eventually he found his way to a new life. A college

degree, a few solid investments that paid off. Somehow, he beat the odds. Somehow, he made a modest success of himself, one he was damned proud of.

With savage pleasure, he'd spent long hours envisioning a time when he would return here and show Mac McGuire how wrong he had been to discount him. When Cassie would see what she had thrown away.

What will you think when you see me now, Cassie? Good enough for you?

The day after the accident, he had called Josh Wheeler from a bus stop in Oklahoma. Nothing that happened to him in the intervening years had ever seemed as scary as waiting for the young rancher to tell him the outcome of Cassie's surgery. After hearing the news that her leg had been saved, Ethan thought he could face anything, including a murky future.

Two weeks later, he'd called Wheeler again. Cassie would soon be moved into rehabilitation; one corner of the ranch house had been outfitted with therapy equipment. She'd probably always have a limp, but she was healing. There wasn't much more Ethan could ask for than that, and in spite of his resentment and anger, he was relieved.

But like a child unable to stop scratching a painful itch, it hadn't been possible to leave it alone. He had to see for himself.

Three months after that disastrous night, Ethan had contacted Josh Wheeler one last time. The man had been a little more distant this time, but he'd eventually told him that Cassie almost never left the Flying M. She had thrown herself into her rehabilitation, and only occasional doctor visits to town interrupted her self-imposed seclusion.

Knowing he would never be welcome by Mac McGuire, Ethan had hitchhiked back to Beaumont and the ranch. He'd walked up to the house without a soul seeing him. Just as he'd been preparing himself to march up to the door and knock, Cassie and her father had come outside. Ethan had slid back into the shelter of trees beside the house and watched as McGuire helped Cassie into the company truck.

She'd said nothing, not even offering one of her dynamic smiles to her father. Her face was thinner, paler. She'd leaned heavily on a cane, and her limp was very pronounced. Once she'd settled in the passenger seat, she had seemed carved out of stone and lost in her own thoughts.

Ethan had no idea where they were headed, but the time was right to approach. He'd step out of the shadows, despite knowing McGuire would pitch a fit. But Ethan had to find a way to talk to Cassie, to *make* her talk to him.

As it happened, no part of his less-than-brilliant idea had panned out. Not because father and daughter had driven away too quickly. Not because McGuire had had him tossed off the property the moment he'd seen him.

It hadn't taken place because Ethan just couldn't do it. He'd stood in the protection of the trees and realized that he couldn't let go of his pride, his sense of being treated unfairly, his anger at being considered unfit to be part of Cassie McGuire's life.

As much as he'd longed to talk to her, he couldn't humiliate himself that way, begging for scraps from people who were no better than he was. He would always regret the part he had played in Cassie's injury, but she was recovering. She obviously didn't need him, didn't want him. It was time he left her alone and moved on.

As the years had passed, he'd deliberately resisted the temptation to check up on her. But now, as he and Meredith reached the front drive to the ranch, he couldn't help wishing he'd at least bothered to do an Internet search or make a few calls. Anything to keep from arriving blind like this.

Two iron arches with winged *M*s announced that they were on McGuire land. It hadn't changed much. Broad pastures spread out behind wooden perimeter fences on either side of the drive. Black-eyed Susans clustered around the base of both entrance posts. Cassie had loved flowers. Had she planted those? Had her recovery been complete enough to allow her that kind of mobility?

Up ahead, the big, handsome house Mac McGuire had built came into view. All log and glass beneath a sky bright and almost tropically blue.

Ethan felt his gut tighten. It was finally here, the moment he had imagined for so long. He could feel excitement flickering through him like an electric current. Something inside him was hungry for this.

"I lived here once," he found himself saying.

"Here?" Meredith asked, turning her head to give him a curious glance. "At the Flying M?"

"When I was twenty-one. Mac McGuire hired me to wrangle stock."

"The place probably hasn't changed much. Although I understand that Cassie's father died some time ago. Since then, she's kept the place running as best she could, considering."

The knot in Ethan's stomach turned into a spasm of dread and panic. It hadn't occurred to him that Mac

McGuire could be dead, and he suddenly didn't want to know what Meredith might tell him about Cassie. "Considering what?" he managed to ask.

"Considering the economy, the hurricanes and the influx of foreign investors who want to turn every bit of ranch land in Texas into shopping malls. Everyone says Cassie's done a great job following in her father's footsteps."

His breath came back. Not a disability, then. "I'm glad everything's worked out well for her."

"Of course, it didn't hurt that her father got her married off before he died."

Ethan looked at the woman sharply as a sinking feeling settled inside him. "She's married." The words sat like stones in his mouth. They didn't belong there.

"Uh-huh," Meredith said. "To someone who can help her run this big ole place. A local rancher, I hear."

CASSIE SLIPPED A doggy treat out of her denim pocket and tossed it toward Ziggy, who caught it with no effort at all. The border collie wolfed it down in one gulp, then sat eagerly waiting for another.

"I don't have any more," Cassie said, showing the dog her empty hands. Ziggy just kept staring at her, tail wagging, mouth shiny with energy and anticipation.

"You're spoiling him," a male voice behind her scolded.

She turned to find Josh approaching from the back porch. He looked handsome in jeans and a pale green, long-sleeved shirt with button-down pocket flaps. His lanky stride was pure Texas cowboy, and even after all these years, she could still admire those slim hips and broad shoulders. He wore his hat, but he'd slipped it back on his head so that she could see the wide smile he gave her.

"That's what I do," she said, as he joined her midway down the outside row of her herb garden.

Leaning over, Josh snapped off a woody stem from a large rosemary bush, releasing the strong aroma. "What are you up to? Mercedes says you've been out here most of the day."

"I've been replanting all afternoon, but when Donny got home he said he wanted to show me something, so I'm just waiting. I'm not sure what he's up to."

"How did he seem?" It was a question they had asked one another a lot in the past few months.

"All right, I suppose. He seemed to think I should be delighted that he got a C on his history exam. He's never going to pass if he doesn't bring his grade up. You know what he said when I told him that?"

"What?"

"'What's the point of studying about the past if you can't change it?'" She straightened, pulling the kinks out of her spine. Her back ached from bending over, and her bad knee was determined to show her who was boss. "I swear, Josh, I wanted to wring his neck. His behavior lately has been deplorable."

"He'll come around. You'll see. He just needs more time."

"I'd feel better about that theory if you hadn't been saying it since last October."

Josh knelt to pluck a few stray leaves from a ragged line of thyme plants. "You worry too much."

She couldn't refute that claim, so she remained silent. But really, why shouldn't she worry? Donny would be thirteen later this year. Puberty. Hormones out of whack.

Mood swings. And on top of that, he was in the midst of the crushing reality that he had not been able to keep his parents from getting a divorce.

Cassie moved along the row of herbs, gathering empty plastic pots, stacking them as she went.

It had been six months since she and Josh had called it quits. Amicably and fairly, without a single harsh word between them. Their breakup had been as civilized as their marriage.

Last year, she'd been the one to broach the subject of divorce after she'd discovered Josh had cheated on her. One time, he'd sworn, and meaningless. But once given an opening, the truth emerged, though Josh had had a hard time articulating the dissatisfaction Cassie had been sensing in him for a long time.

"You know I love you, Cassandra," he had said sadly. "I always have. I thought it would be enough for us to start from there. But let's face it. You've never felt the same about me. And over the years, there are times…I can't help thinking maybe…what if…I want a house-ful of kids. And I don't want to be too old to enjoy them…"

As though ashamed to have such thoughts, he had looked away. Personally, Cassie could have wept at his honesty. She'd never been unfaithful in all her married years, but that didn't mean she hadn't entertained some pretty unwifely thoughts. Josh was too good for her. Too nice. It made her want to behave badly just to see if he could be pushed into passion.

Well-mannered coupling with him had left her feeling cheated, and the man had never stirred more than feelings of deep friendship in her. She didn't know why. It was just a fact, like the sun rising tomorrow.

For years she had tried not to think about the only other man she had ever made love to. Tried not to recall those times when she had kissed Ethan Rafferty and his mere touch had been the end of decency and good manners. Going there only brought back a memory of grief and pain so raw that she could hardly breathe.

Not that it mattered much whether she consciously thought of Ethan or not. She had the constant reminder of him in their son—Donny's dark hair and sky-blue eyes. That devilish twist to his lips when he was up to mischief. God must have a sense of humor, after all, to give her a child who looked so much like his father.

Thinking of her son, Cassie scanned the land behind the house. The yard ended at the beaten trail that ran from the side of the house to the barns. Beyond the trail, fenced paddocks held a few horses that munched grass contentedly. There was no sign of Donny.

The afternoon sun was brutal on her back, and she wanted nothing more than to strip off her clothes and slip into the tub for a soothing soak. Where *was* he? And what was he up to?

Josh had followed her down the row and now stopped in front of her. His hand touched her cheek, and she caught the scent of sweet, pungent thyme. "You have dirt on your nose," he said, swiping his finger across it.

She didn't pull away. Their relationship had always been so easy, so uncomplicated. His brief fling hadn't changed that. Neither had divorce. And no matter what, he was still a wonderful father to Donny.

He glanced over her shoulder as Ziggy began to bark. Cassie turned to see what had caught their attention.

A man and woman were coming around the corner of

the house. They were no more than silhouettes because of the rusty light of the lowering sun behind them. Cassie squinted and shaded her eyes, waiting.

The woman wore typical Texas casual, and Cassie thought she looked familiar. A Realtor, maybe. *Melody? Meredith?* Yes, that was the name.

As for the man, he was dressed in a suit, distinctly out of place here amid longhorns and chaps. Cassie supposed he could be a businessman from Houston, but even in the city the men wore boots and Stetsons. He looked...

She pulled in a sudden, shocked breath. She felt as though she'd been kicked, hard and fast. Josh must have heard her, or sensed her stiffening, because his arm came around her possessively, protectively.

Ethan.

Here. Back on Flying M property.

The man who had made her heart slip again and again into overdrive. The man who had helped to shape her entire existence. The man who had given her Donny, the most precious thing in her life.

How could he be walking toward her this very minute? How could the fragile universe she'd created for herself crumble so quickly?

Some animal instinct briefly flared, then just as quickly burned out. Disgusted by her reaction, Cassie forced herself to draw a deep, fortifying breath, while sanity made a welcome return.

She could handle this. No need to let old memories stir and ridiculous hungers awaken. She was no longer a lovesick eighteen-year-old girl. Lovesick. Even now, the word made her cringe when she remembered how foolish she'd been thirteen years ago.

"Ziggy!" she admonished the dog, who immediately began running silently in happy circles.

The couple reached them. The blonde held out her hand. "Hello there! Your housekeeper said everyone was out back. I hope you don't mind if we join you." She handed Josh her business card, offering him a big smile. "Do you remember me from the last town meeting? I'm Meredith Summerlin, from Summerlin Realty."

"Yes," Josh said. "Nice to see you again."

Meredith indicated her companion. "This is my client, Ethan Rafferty. He says he used to work on the Flying M years ago."

Josh nodded. "Of course we remember him."

Something in her ex-husband's tone told her that he was just as surprised as she was, but Cassie couldn't have glanced at him if her life depended on it. She had not been able to stop looking at Ethan, no matter how determined she was to remain composed. The truth was, her heart was racing, and she couldn't make it slow down.

"It's nice to see you both again," Ethan said politely, and held out his hand.

She took it. What else could she do, really? She was dimly aware that his calluses and nicked knuckles had disappeared. He carried himself well, and his muscular body seemed honed to new hardness. Every inch of him looked sophisticated, tamed, important.

"Hello, Ethan," she said simply, keeping her tone neutral even though her nerves were a jumbled mess.

He gave her a quick smile as if he appreciated and even admired her attempt at indifference. Then his features were unreadable once more.

Thank God Meredith Summerlin was in full business mode. "Mr. Rafferty's interested in the acreage you have for sale off Jackalope Road. I was wondering if we could sit down sometime soon and discuss the particulars."

Cassie frowned at Ethan. "You want to ranch that land?"

"No, that's not—"

"Mom! Dad!" a distant voice shouted. "Check it out!"

Everyone turned to see a palomino come flying around the corner of the house, ridden along the grassy trail by a boy who waved wildly at them.

It was Donny, on his new gelding, Cochise. He'd had the animal less than two weeks—a surprise present from Josh because he'd outgrown his older mount. Cassie didn't think the two were used to one another yet, and she wished Donny would take things more slowly. Right now, he had the reins clenched in his teeth as he spread his arms wide and guided Cochise only with his legs, like a rider in a Wild West show.

A wave of tenderness for so lively and charming a child ran through her, but she couldn't help that her heart jumped a little. *Be careful,* she wanted to shout. *Don't you know what can happen?*

Then, just like that, a different kind of panic zoomed up her spine. A fluttering sensation spread out from her abdomen. If Donny came any closer, Ethan was sure to notice the resemblance. He would see his own features in his son's face.

He would know the truth.

"Way to go, Donny!" Josh yelled, clapping his hands. Ziggy began barking his support, too.

Cassie kept silent, trying to think what to do.

Donny and Josh often accused her of being too protective. Having put up with her father's smothering concern for so long, she had never wanted to be that way, but she knew how quickly things could go wrong.

And yet you couldn't grow up on a working ranch without spending hours in the saddle. Donny had been on horses since he was a toddler. Josh had seen to that, and he was right. Her incident with Bandera mustn't be allowed to poison the boy.

Could she play the "worried mother" card? Not difficult to do since her son often frightened her with his antics these days.

Yes, definitely. *Now.*

"Donny!" she called. "Enough. Put Cochise away and—"

"That was nothing," the boy said. "Watch this!"

He urged the palomino into a tight, circling canter, kicked his feet out of the stirrups, then swung himself around in the saddle until he was mounted backward.

Really frightened for him now, Cassie made a move in his direction. "Stop that right now."

"But, Mom—"

Josh caught her arm. "Cassandra—"

"I said stop!"

Donny pulled the horse to a halt, slipped frontward again easily, then began walking Cochise toward them.

Cassie's facial muscles froze as he approached. She spun around, understanding that radical change could come to her life in a heartbeat. She searched Ethan's face for any glimpse of recognition. His eyes were on Donny, but she couldn't spot the slightest shift of interest in him.

"It looks like you've got a daredevil on your hands," she heard Meredith say mildly.

Obviously feeling thwarted, Donny slumped in the saddle like a beaten warrior. "I can't do anything around here!"

Cassie turned back to him. "Put Cochise away and go inside," she snapped. The last thing she wanted was for the boy to come any closer. "Feed Ziggy and take your bath. We'll talk later."

As though sensing Cassie's tension, Meredith spoke up, offering a light laugh. "Kids! They can really make you want to pull your hair out, can't they?"

"I'm sorry," Cassie said, her heart starting to settle at last as her son headed off toward the horse barn. She pulled in a deep breath. "We were discussing the property..." The words rose clear and steady from a throat she would have sworn was paralyzed.

"Yes, we were," Ethan said. Nothing showed on his face. Nothing had to. The too quiet, too silky timbre of his voice said it all. "I thought we might agree on a price for the property fairly quickly. But now—" his eyes followed Donny's departing figure "—it appears there may be something else we have to negotiate."

CHAPTER FOUR

BY THE TIME ETHAN PULLED into the parking lot of his hotel, he was ninety-nine percent certain he had a handle on the situation.

He had a son. A son he'd never known existed.

But that didn't mean his world had to be turned upside down.

This sort of thing happened sometimes. People made mistakes, lost control. You couldn't always erase what you'd done. Sometimes, no matter what you planned, you had to live with the consequences of your actions. Hadn't he learned that years ago, the hard way?

So here was a new challenge. A big one. But he knew he'd find a way to manage it. So what if this was Cassie's turf, and she had the home field advantage? They could still work this out. Calmly. Reasonably. He'd call his attorney, see what his options and responsibilities were. Cassie didn't need to worry. He had no desire to play daddy. This didn't have to impact his game plan for the future. Not one damned bit.

Yanking off his tie, Ethan threw it onto the passenger seat. He caught his eyes in the rearview mirror. *Who do you think you're kidding, Rafferty?*

Just that quickly, his life was on a different track, like a train careening off its course. He had a kid, a twelve-year-old handful by the looks of it. A child who was so much a younger version of Ethan that he could have been looking in a time-traveler's mirror.

Unwanted emotions churned through him, feelings he couldn't even put a name to.

My son.

Mine.

He sat in the silence of the parking lot, listening to the ticking of the car's engine as it cooled. For just a few moments, a hard knuckle of anger sent a jolt through his body.

Why had Cassie kept him in the dark all these years? How did she dare? By what right…?

Restraint shattered inside him. Only one way to find out.

Ethan threw the rental car in Reverse, heading back toward the I-10 and the Flying M Ranch.

WHEN HE STOOD AT THE ranch's front door, he was a little calmer, but not by much.

There were questions he wanted answers to, but he wasn't likely to get them if he came charging in full of righteous indignation. Conquering the impulse to pound his fist on the thick wood, Ethan drew a huge breath and knocked with all the practical determination of a traveling salesman.

He wasn't expecting Cassie to answer. A housekeeper had led them to the backyard earlier that afternoon, but when the door swung wide, it wasn't either woman.

It was Donny.

For a moment Ethan was completely tongue-tied, something that rarely happened to him anymore. He felt slightly breathless, as though he'd been jogging. Worst of all, he couldn't seem to stop staring.

The boy, either uncomfortable under Ethan's scrutiny or simply impatient, shifted. He jerked his chin up in acknowledgment.

"Hey," he said without any particular grace. "You're the guy who was here earlier."

"Yes," Ethan answered. "And you're Donny." Named after Cassie's old man, he supposed. He wondered what would happen if he added, "And I'm your father."

But of course he said nothing like that. Instead, he gave the boy a smile. "Are your parents home? I'd like to speak with them."

"Dad's staying at River Bottom. Mom's in the Torture Chamber."

Josh was staying at his parents' old place, instead of here with Cassie? What did that mean?

Ethan lifted one brow. "Your mother's in the Torture Chamber?"

"It's just a gym, but that's what she calls it. She hits the hot tub almost every night, but she should be out soon."

Ethan enjoyed a fast, private fantasy about how Cassie would look relaxing in bubbling, steamy water up to the swell of her breasts. He might be furious with her, but when he'd first seen her this afternoon, it had pained him to accept the brutal truth. Over the years he had convinced himself that she meant nothing to him anymore, but his body, his senses, seemed to have remained infatuated.

It annoyed him that just the sight of her could still pack that kind of wallop. He shut those thoughts down before they could take hold. "Can I wait?"

"I guess," Donny answered with a shrug.

The kid led him across the oak-floored foyer, into

what Ethan remembered as the living room. It looked the same as when Mac McGuire had been alive. Lots of heavy furnishings, a high-end Western theme courtesy of Neiman Marcus. Leather and suede and beaten iron.

Ethan moved to the center of the room, then turned toward his son. Donny was slipping into a denim jacket. The dog Ethan had seen earlier came up to join them, and the boy leaned down to give its head a scratch.

"I gotta go," he said. "You can park it here until Mom gets out. Will you tell her I'm going for a walk? We're just going down to the pond. I like to look at the moon on the water while Zig chases frogs."

Something in the boy's tone made suspicion blossom in Ethan's mind. Before he could stop himself he asked, "Is that really where you're headed?"

Donny's posture developed a distinctly offended stance. His jaw looked rock solid. "Dude, are you calling me a liar?"

Not a very good start, Rafferty. Ethan raised his hands in mock surrender. "Sorry. I was young once, and too many details always made my mother suspicious. You need to keep it simple."

Hot color swam in Donny's cheeks. There was a long moment of silence while the boy nibbled at his bottom lip uncertainly and swept his gaze over Ethan.

Finally, he said awkwardly, "Okay, I'm going down to the barn to see my new horse. I'm just hanging out with him, though. No riding in the dark, no messing around trying to teach him tricks. So Mom doesn't need to freak out. Tell her that. But only if she asks where I am. Deal?"

"Seems fair."

As though satisfied, Donny nodded and snapped his fingers at the dog. "Come on, Zig."

Before he could get to the doorway, Ethan called out, "Hold on a minute."

Donny blew out an audible sigh as he turned. Were all twelve-year-old boys like this? How would Ethan know? He'd never spent much time around children, so he had virtually nothing for comparison.

"Would you mind telling your mother I'm here?"

The boy left the room, and Ethan heard him tromping heavy-footed down the hallway.

A few moments later, he heard Donny shout, "Mom! You got company!"

Ethan couldn't hear a response over the sound of Donny talking to the dog and his boots returning to the living room. His hands were shoved into his pockets, but just before he turned to leave with Ziggy at his heels, he seemed to remember his manners.

"You want anything?" he asked. "Water? Iced tea?"

Answers, kid. That's what I want. But all Ethan did was politely decline. In another moment, the boy banged out the front door, and he was alone in the Flying M's living room.

The place was tomb-quiet, as though brooding about the crisis threatening its owner. He'd only been in the ranch house a few times, and he'd forgotten how big it was. Impersonal and stiff in spite of the massive fireplace and warm, earthy colors. Back in Colorado Springs, he'd built an entire cabin for himself that wasn't much bigger than this room.

No wonder Cassie had decided he wouldn't fit in here. It was true.

To keep himself occupied while he waited, he roamed the room, trying to admire Tim Cox paintings and Remington sculptures that spoke of wealth in a Western world. The Flying M must still be doing all right. Mac McGuire's little girl didn't seem to have lost her father's fortune over the years.

Of course, she'd had a husband to help her.

A long bookcase stood against one wall. Ethan stopped in front of it, remembering that trophies had been displayed here once. Now it was full of memorabilia and framed pictures.

He studied the lineup of photographs. Cassie's father, astride a black stallion. A shot of Josh Wheeler, shaking hands, accepting an award from some organization. His parents were here, too—a younger version of Josh standing between them in cap and gown.

Gradually the pictures became more current, and Ethan immediately realized that it had been a mistake to wander over here.

Josh with Donny astride his first horse. Cassie and a younger Donny opening Christmas presents in front of a towering fir. School photos. Vacations. There was one of the three of them at a football game, the confident young family linked together by laughter. Josh Wheeler's arm was draped around each of them. Cassie's head lay against his shoulder and a gap-toothed Donny grinned up at them both.

The three of them. Tight-knit. Loving. Perfect.

To his surprise, Ethan felt a cold hand seize his heart as he replaced the photograph. The pure pain of time lost exploded within his chest. Twelve years of missed opportunities. Twelve years of memories from a boy's childhood that could never be re-created. Ethan's son didn't know him from Adam.

Deep inside, there was the cruel, bleak knowledge that Donny had grown up calling Josh Wheeler "Dad."

Ethan moved away from the bookcase. Now that he knew about Donny, how difficult would it be to make things right? How long would it take? And what was "right," anyway?

His gut told him with dark certainty that, whatever lay ahead, it was bound to be hard and painful for everyone.

He looked at his watch. It had been ten minutes. What was keeping her? Did she think if she stalled long enough he might go away and never come back? Was she afraid to face him? Or was she simply making him wait to show who was in charge here?

Whatever her reasons, it only made him more angry. And more determined than ever to get some answers.

CASSIE PLUCKED THE headphones out of her ears and slid her iPod into the basket beside her therapy pool. Then she slid lower into the tub until the hot, bubbling water tickled her chin. A satisfied sigh escaped her lips. After a day like today, she needed this. Not just to soak away her body's stiffness, but to calm her nerves and soothe the tension that made her every muscle feel as though it had been attached to a live wire.

She lifted her bad leg, letting it rest against the side of the tub. The flesh was crisscrossed and puckered with surgical scars even after all these years. That night in the barn, everything had shattered Humpty Dumpty style. The pieces had been put back together again, but the doctor could only do so much. It wasn't pretty, and no matter how diligently Cassie worked out in this room, it never would be.

With a frown, she slipped her leg back under the hot water. She had never allowed herself extended forays into the deep end of the pity pool, and there was no reason to start now. Forget aches in the winter and pain when she stood too long in one place. Her body was whole. She'd been so incredibly lucky.

Lucky.

She drew a shaky breath and, for the first time in ages, let her mind run freely over the night of her accident.

The time spent in Bandera's stall was still a blank to her, and what came afterward at the hospital was no more than flashes, snapshots of pain and fear. A nurse trying to keep her awake. Vital signs. Her father weeping over her.

Most of the memories refused to mesh, but the sound of the doctor's voice had somehow sliced through her haze. Asking permission to take her leg if it proved necessary to save her life. She had felt her insides shut down with the shock of that possibility, with the fear that even if she lived she would never be the same.

By the time Ethan had come to her, she had known what she had to do. They couldn't marry. It would be so wrong to tie a virile, exciting man like Ethan Rafferty to a cripple. Their plans of travel, adventure, of starting a new, exhilarating life together—all of it disappeared like smoke as she lay there feeling the pain medication take hold. Dreams were fine for those who had some hope of attaining them. But starting that moment, she didn't have that hope.

He had kissed her, an achingly gentle touch of his mouth against hers. She'd fought to stay conscious, to ignore the sweet, rough purr of his voice promising that everything would be all right. She had made herself concentrate on her breathing. One slow, even breath. Another.

And somehow, she had told him to go. She'd told him that she blamed him for what had happened. That he wasn't right for her.

That she never wanted to see him again.

Now, it seemed so foolish to think that had been the end of it. Twenty-four hours later, when she had awakened to find her leg still intact, though permanently damaged, the doctor had informed her that she was pregnant. She might have managed to keep Ethan from throwing his life away, but hers had been altered forever.

Looking back, she remembered being terrified momentarily at the idea of becoming a single mother. Yet at the same time she had felt something light and airy travel through her.

Ethan's child.

It didn't matter that her father was horrified and angered by the news. It didn't matter that her pregnancy would make the long, torturous months of therapy that lay ahead that much more difficult. Her heart reeled with the sweetness of it, willing to snatch at any crumb. The blaze of light within her was too beautiful and dazzling to be extinguished.

Slipping her hand beneath the water in the tub, Cassie ran her fingers over her submerged belly, remembering the way it had looked when she had been carrying Donny. It seemed like only yesterday that she had held her son for the first time, and Ethan's imprint on that tiny face had been so clear.

Not once had she ever regretted the decision to have

her baby. From the moment of his birth, Donny had become the fulcrum upon which her life was balanced. And never, ever, would she allow Ethan's reappearance in her life to change that.

All her protective instincts were humming. She would find a way to handle this latest development. Josh would help her. Together they would protect Donny from anything Ethan might have in mind. She just wished she knew what it was.

Cassie inched down again, until the curve of her neck rested against the back of the tub. She closed her eyes, concentrating on taking deep, calming breaths, wishing her mind would stop ping-ponging back and forth with a dozen possibilities.

Maybe, as Josh had suggested, they were worrying needlessly. Who could guess what Ethan had in mind? He had come back to Beaumont on business. Obviously he had plans for the future. Wasn't it possible that he had no interest in establishing a real relationship with his son? Were they contractually obligated to sell that Jackalope land to him?

Maybe he had a wife and children of his own someplace. No reason he shouldn't after all this time. She tried to envision it, and discovered that she couldn't. He had been an only child, a loner all his life. Hadn't he once told her that, given his parents' history of creating the most undesirable home life possible, he could not imagine ever having children?

Stop it. Everything will be okay. You're worrying for nothing.

She heard the Torture Chamber's door open. Since Mercedes had already left for the day, and Josh had moved back to River Bottom, it had to be Donny. She

loved him beyond life, but lately he'd developed a dis-
obedient streak designed to annoy the heck out of her.
She refused to open her eyes and give him her attention
until he behaved like the gentleman she had raised him
to be.

"What happened to your manners?" she asked him
over the sound of the bubbling water. "Go back outside
and knock. Just because you live in this house doesn't
give you the right to trample my privacy."

"Considering what I learned today, it seems strange
to hear you talk about respecting a person's rights."

Startled, Cassie snapped her eyes open. She sat upright so fast that water splashed over the edge of the tub
and one shoulder strap of her swimsuit slid down her
arm.

Ethan stood in the doorway. He was still dressed in
the suit she'd seen him in earlier, minus the tie. His
collar lay open at the throat, but other than that, he
looked every bit the successful businessman.

She'd barely been able to look at him that afternoon,
and the setting sun had helped to mask his features. Now
she saw that he was still the handsome heartbreaker. The
deep-set eyes she had fought to forget were still the same
intense shade of blue, the jaw still strong and square and
fiercely proud.

But there *were* some changes. The light caught a few
silver threads in his dark hair, and it was no longer the
reckless tumble she had once loved to run her fingers
through. She supposed it was his mouth that had changed
the most. No longer cocky and inviting. It was cast in
such a somber line right now, so taut she could never
imagine it smiling.

He came to the edge of the tub and stared down at

her. He seemed taller than ever and she felt foolish, off center. Two feelings she abhorred.

She lifted her chin. She would be strong for Donny's sake, just as she'd made herself be strong during those first terrible months of her pregnancy. "What are you doing here, Ethan?" she managed to ask.

One brow spiked. "You can't guess?"

"Get out."

"We need to talk."

Her heart leaped, then took on a faster rhythm. She slipped her swimsuit strap back up her arm and set her jaw. "This isn't the time or place. It's been a long day and I'm not up to—"

"Get up to it, then," he interrupted harshly. "Because I'm not leaving until I get a few answers."

Her robe lay on a nearby stool. He scooped it up and tossed it to her. She caught it before the material had a chance to slip into the water. Ethan sat down while she stood and belted the terry cloth around her.

Cassie settled for sitting on the lip of the tub where the tiles were widest. Although she felt at a distinct disadvantage, she worked hard to keep her gaze steady. "You were always arrogant and full of yourself," she commented. "But I don't remember you being so insensitive."

He shrugged. "I guess you'd know all about being insensitive. Giving birth to my son and keeping it a secret from me ranks right up there as damned unfeeling."

A sudden flare of guilt made her anger spike hotly in defense. "Donny is not your son. The fact that you supplied the sperm is nothing more than biology. So don't come in here demanding apologies."

"Right now, I'm demanding nothing but a few simple

answers. We can talk this out, or I can have my lawyer contact your lawyer and let all hell break loose. Is that really how you want to play this?"

She drew a harsh breath, trying to hold on to her control. "You'd do that to Donny? You'd destroy his life in a court battle?"

"Stop looking at me like you're trying to decide which limb to chew off. I don't want to destroy anything, and that's why I'm here. I need answers."

His tone had softened a little, but his look held no charity. It turned her heart over with fear and dread. If she let him into this part of her life, there would be no going back. But what else could she do?

"What do you want to know?" she asked in a subdued voice.

"For starters, how this happened. No, forget that. So much for protection, I guess. What I want to know is how you ended up raising my child and never bothering to contact me. Did you hate me that much?"

She blinked in surprise. "It had nothing to do with hating you," she told him, holding his gaze with straight-forward honesty.

"Then talk to me, Cassie."

She could feel his desperate interest, his inquiry, the power of it. She licked her lips and choked down the anger that would accomplish nothing. "Apparently, the last tests before surgery showed I was pregnant. I was almost under by then, and there were bigger issues for the doctor to deal with. They didn't tell me about the baby until afterward, when I was out of the woods."

Ethan nodded slowly, as though digesting the information. "I'd left the state by then."

She nodded. "There was nothing I could do about it at

first. I told my father the day he brought me home from the hospital. You can imagine how well he took it."

"Did either of you think about telling me?"

"At the time I was a little busy trying to make sure I could walk again."

The words, she could see immediately, wounded him. His eyes left her face to play over her body. The robe hid her bad leg, but she still felt self-conscious.

Silence fell between them. Finally, his eyes found hers again. "How bad was it?"

She wasn't ready for his pity. She didn't want it. Her stomach felt like warm lead, but she refused to give in to another bout of nerves. "The surgery was successful. I had a great physical therapist who never let me slack for a moment. I managed."

He looked around, taking in the various pieces of equipment that had helped her maintain mobility for years—parallel bars, a treadmill, leg weights that challenged her every day. Her father had created this haven with all the state-of-the-art apparatus available at the time. Long ago she had dubbed this room the Torture Chamber, but the truth was, she'd come to love it. This was *her* place, where she could push herself to the limit or sit quietly and think. Even cry her eyes out if she wanted to.

"Does all this stuff really make a difference?" Ethan asked.

"Yes. I only limp a little if I've had a particularly stressful day."

"I guess this would qualify as one of them."

Another uncomfortable moment or two passed. She remembered that they had once been good with silence, but now it seemed oppressive.

Then suddenly, he looked into her eyes again, and Cassie's world threatened to teeter.

What had made her think she could sit face-to-face with Ethan without remembering the demand of his hard mouth? Or the crush of that body on hers? She felt beyond anger. Beyond exhaustion. She wasn't sure where she was anymore, but not since she'd held Donny in her arms as a baby had she felt such turbulent, contradictory emotions.

She swiped a few damp locks of hair away from her face, sighing heavily. "Look," she said. "I'm not completely heartless. I know the accident was as much my fault as yours. While I was recovering, I asked my father to do everything he could to find you, and it was only after I began to get around well on my own that I realized he hadn't tried very hard."

A half smile touched Ethan's lips. "I can't imagine he would have, given his feelings about me."

"For a long time I didn't see anyone but doctors and therapists. I stayed here. I couldn't just leave and try to find you on my own. By the time I could start a real search, I was six months along with Donny. Dad didn't approve, of course, but I insisted we try. For the baby's sake," she added quickly, just in case Ethan got the wrong idea. "I was able to track you as far as Arizona, but after that…you just seemed to disappear."

He looked down, moving restlessly on his chair. Cassie watched the muscles in his jaw flex. "After we spoke at the hospital…I was pretty determined not to be found," he conceded. "I worked a lot of jobs no one else wanted, where you can disappear off the face of the earth and no one questions why you want to be there."

"Anything to get away from me, I guess," she said softly.

"Those kinds of jobs pay well, and…yes. I wanted to be as far away from this place as possible."

"That may have worked for you, Ethan, but it didn't help me any."

His head jerked up, and he pinned her with a sharp look. "So you just decided to marry the first man you could find to fit the bill, and let him be the baby's father for the next twelve years?"

"It wasn't like that. I was pregnant and trying to put my life back together. You know Josh has always been a good friend to me. He was here a lot, helping me every step of the way. He celebrated my successes and…kept me from giving up when I couldn't see any reason to go on. He's the most kindhearted, generous man I know, and I owe him a debt I could never repay."

Something dark crossed Ethan's features. There was a coiled tension about him now that Cassie could sense even from the distance that separated them. He shifted again, as though trying to lessen it. "You married him as a way of saying thank-you? What was in it for him?"

Under the brutal directness of his gaze, she swallowed hard, but tried to put steel in her tone. "I'm telling you what I did after I found out I was going to have your baby. But that's all I'm going to say about my marriage to Josh. Frankly, it's none of your business."

"But Donny is," he replied with a touch of belligerence.

"He doesn't have to be."

"What's that supposed to mean?"

"Josh and I have talked. Nothing has to change if

you're willing to just leave it alone. Josh is Donny's father in every way."

"Not by blood, he's not."

"Fatherhood is about a lot more than that."

"Cass—"

Searching for the advantage, Cassie slipped off the side of the tub and went to him. They were suddenly face-to-face, and she was determined not to be intimidated. "Josh adopted Donny when he was a baby."

She could see that took him back a little. After a while he asked, "Does Donny know Josh isn't his real father?"

"Yes. But he loves Josh. So you could turn your back on this, and no one would be the wiser. You don't have to feel obligated—"

"Obligated?" Ethan snapped, his voice full of indignation. "Is that all you think I feel?"

Cassie shook her head, desperate to get through to him without souring their relationship completely. For Donny's sake, she needed to keep it civil. "I can't pretend to understand everything you feel right now. Shocked, I guess. Angry with me for not telling you. Even wanting revenge, maybe. But you can't tell me that suddenly you're in the mood to become a father. You don't want children. Especially not a prepubescent boy who thinks he knows more than every adult around him."

Ethan frowned. "Who said I don't want kids?"

"You did," she replied, surprised that he didn't remember. "Years ago. You told me that after the miserable job your parents had done raising you, you couldn't imagine having kids of your own. So do you have any? Do you have a wife and a bunch of little ones waiting for you somewhere?"

"No."

"And now suddenly you want a son?"

"I don't have to *want* a son," he growled at her. "I have one."

Frustrated, Cassie shook her head. "What about your plans for the future? Meredith Summerlin mentioned that you want our land in order to grow your business. Whatever that involves, do you really need this complication right now?"

He snorted a short laugh. "You really don't want me in his life, do you?"

She swung away. "I will do anything to keep Donny from getting hurt."

"So you think the easiest thing for everyone is for me to just pretend I never met him?"

"Yes. Take your anger out on me if you want, but don't hurt Donny. He's been through so much in the past year."

"What do you mean, 'so much'?"

She licked her bottom lip. Might as well tell him the truth, if he hadn't heard it already. He was bound to sooner or later. "Josh and I divorced a few months ago. Donny's taking it very hard."

Ethan didn't try to hide his disdain. "I thought he was your knight in shining armor. The man who made life worth living again."

Their gazes locked like crossed sabers. She refused to speak.

"Sorry," he said at last, though they both knew he wasn't. He stood up and moved toward the door. "I realize that the timing could be better, but that doesn't change anything. I have a right to know my own son."

"Ethan—"

When his hand was on the doorknob, he turned back to face her. "Do what you have to do, Cassie," he said in a quietly determined voice. "But understand one thing. As far as Donny's future is concerned, I'm not going to just quietly disappear."

CHAPTER FIVE

EARLY THE NEXT MORNING Cassie drove over to River Bottom. The ranch that Josh's parents had built lay only a mile from the Flying M. Less than that, if you took some of the trails through the woods, but after spending a sleepless night, Cassie didn't feel like making the effort on foot. She wanted to talk to Josh as soon as possible about the visit she'd had from Ethan.

She expected to find him in his mother's old sunroom, sipping coffee from his favorite mug. They had loved days like this. Warm sunshine, with the feeling that spring had firmly taken hold at last.

Instead, as soon as she got out of the ranch truck she heard the most awful racket coming from the backyard. When she rounded the corner of the house, she was surprised to see Josh stripped to the waist and sweating in the morning sun. He stood next to an enormous wood chipper that emitted a buzzing screech every time he tossed a tree limb into it.

And there were a *lot* of limbs.

Two years ago Hurricane Enid had ripped through this part of Texas. The massive oak behind the ranch house had fallen, taking a good portion of the old garden with it. Since no one lived at his parents' place anymore, there had been no hurry to remove it. But when Josh had moved back to River Bottom after the divorce, he'd mentioned that he wanted to get the place in working order. Nevertheless, she was surprised that he had decided today was the perfect time to tackle this particular project.

Because of the noise, Josh hadn't heard her approach. She tapped him on the shoulder, wincing from the racket as he fed another big limb into the chipper.

Startled, he swung around. His lips were tight, but he managed a small smile. Removing one work glove, he pulled earplugs out of his ears. With no limbs to munch on, the chipper settled into a noisy hum.

Cassie motioned toward the downed tree. "I thought you were going to pay someone to do this."

"No reason why I can't handle it." He scooped up a few stray branches, then tossed them into the chipper. "Besides," he shouted over the roar of the machinery, "I kind of like the idea of seeing something go from being a big pain in the butt to sawdust in three seconds flat."

"Can you turn it off?" Cassie asked, clapping her hands over her ears.

Josh flipped a switch and silence dropped into place. He removed his other glove, then tucked both of them into the back of his jeans. Cassie shook her head at him.

"What's that for?" he asked.

"You're wasting your time. It won't work, you know. You feed Ethan into a wood chipper, the cops are bound to come asking questions."

Josh wiggled his brows at her. "But he'd still be out of our hair."

She watched his jaw tighten and knew that he was thinking the same thing she was. What were they going to do about Ethan? What *could* they do?

"He came to see me last night," she told him.

"You should have called me."

"No time. It was a surprise visit."

Josh grimaced. "Still the same guy, I see. Doing what he darned well pleases."

"You can't really blame him, can you? He wanted answers."

Josh tilted his head, frowning. "Did he win you over that quickly?"

She frowned back. "Of course he didn't. Stop acting like a jealous husband."

He left that challenge unanswered. They both knew there was no truth to it—there hadn't been that kind of passion between them for years. Maybe there never had been, really. One of the things that had made her finally suggest a divorce was the fact that when Josh had cheated on her, it hadn't been the heartbreaker it should have been. Not for a man you truly loved.

"How did it go?" he asked at last. "Are you all right?"

"Yes. He made me mad as hell, but once I got past the shock of seeing him again, we were able to keep it civil."

Just barely, she added to herself. She couldn't admit, even to Josh, how much that sudden reunion with Ethan had bruised her confidence in her ability to handle any challenge that confronted her.

After she gave Josh a bald outline of what had happened, he still looked unsatisfied. "Did he say what he intends to do?"

"Not really. Obviously he wants to know Donny better. If the situation were reversed, wouldn't you?"

Josh looked so miserable, so tense. His lips were a

grim line again, and as though he couldn't discuss it anymore, he turned and began gathering more tree limbs. It pained her to see him this way. He was a good man who didn't deserve this.

She'd been so upset over what Ethan's reappearance might mean to her, she'd forgotten who would be the real victim here. Josh was not a blood relation to Donny, but he'd been his father in every way. He mustn't be shut out, no matter what.

Wanting desperately to comfort him, she caught his arm so that he had to face her again. She managed a wan smile. "We can handle this, Josh. We can. And if we can't—" she slid a glance toward the wood chipper "—there's always plan B."

Josh shoved the limbs into the maw of the silent chipper. Brushing his hands together, he gave her a determined shake of his head. "I'm not going to let him cut me out of Donny's life, Cassandra."

"Surely he'd never do that. And I won't let him. *You're* Donny's father, and he loves you so much."

After a moment or two, Josh slanted her a thoughtful look. "So what now?" he asked, his voice scratchy and a couple of tones deeper than usual. "We sell him that land, he'll be back in our lives."

"What difference does selling him the land really make? We can't let him think we're afraid of him. The Realtor said he's offering cash up front, and I could certainly make use of it. Besides, if we refuse, knowing Ethan, he'll just find another plot close by. Lots of For Sale signs out there these days."

"I still don't like it."

"I know," she said, rubbing her hand up and down his arm. "But we have to keep this from turning into a war. If he wants to get to know Donny better, I think we should let him. No word to Donny, of course, about who Ethan really is. But why don't we invite him to dinner? Let him see what a charmer Donny can be."

Josh snorted, and for the first time since she'd come, he gave her a real smile. "Given Donny's behavior lately, that ought to have Rafferty running for the hills."

I wish I thought it would be that easy. She remembered how determined Ethan could be. Once he set his mind to something, he'd never give up without a fight. Although, come to think of it, he'd given up pretty quickly on her. But this was his son.

She tossed Josh her most reassuring grin and pulled her cell phone from the pocket of her jeans. She punched in the phone number from the business card Meredith Summerlin had given her yesterday. As soon as the real estate agent came on the line, she hit the speakerphone button so Josh could hear the conversation.

"Hello, Ms. Summerlin. It's Cassandra and Josh Wheeler."

"Hello there!" the woman exclaimed enthusiastically. "What a coincidence. I was going to call you later this morning."

"I was wondering if you could do me a favor. Would you happen to know where Mr. Rafferty's staying? I'd like to get in touch with him."

"He was at the Crockett, but that's why I was going to call. Mr. Rafferty has had to return suddenly to Colorado Springs. That's where he's from, I believe."

"I see," Cassie said, exchanging a frown with Josh. *Now what?* "Nothing serious, I hope."

"I don't think so. He mentioned something about

having to keep an important appointment with his attorney."

Cassie stiffened, and, beside her, Josh turned away with a muttered curse.

"But I wanted to reassure you," Meredith Summerlin went on. "He's eager to go to contract on that property, and I'll have the papers ready for you to sign by tomorrow, assuming my connection in the title office comes through. You could have money in escrow by the end of this week."

"Oh," Cassie said. "That quickly."

She finished the call to Meredith, then shut the cell phone with a quiet snap. Ethan could be her neighbor soon. But more importantly, she could guess what that meeting in Colorado Springs would be about. He wasn't wasting any time finding out what his options were with Donny.

She glanced toward the wood chipper. Maybe plan B would be the best answer to this mess, after all.

QUINTIN AVONACO TOOK A long swig from his iced tea glass, then set it down on the porch railing. "You want to know what I think?"

Ethan met his partner's gaze squarely. "No, but that never stops you from telling me."

Eight years had passed since they'd shared a hospital room in Denver. Ethan had been forced there to have his inflamed appendix removed, while Quintin, a regular on the rodeo circuit, had gotten the stuffing stomped out of him by an ornery bull named Hellraiser. They had recognized each other as kindred spirits immediately—two men driven by the desire for a better life and finding it just beyond their grasp.

They both hated hospitals, had an almost reverential admiration for the Eagles' music, loved Broncos football and thought asparagus was the nastiest vegetable on the planet. By the time Ethan had been discharged, they were friends. A year later, when he had accrued enough money to get Horse Sense up and running—if barely—Ethan had known just who he wanted to have working at his side.

From the front door of the cabin, they could see most of the paddocks. Quintin squinted toward Ethan's bay gelding, Houdini, who stood placidly soaking up the afternoon sun. "I think," he said evenly, "Mrs. Wheeler's still a burr under your saddle. And not in the pain-in-the-ass kind of way, either. In the I-can't-forget-her kind of way."

Ethan leaned back in one of the porch chairs and didn't respond. He took another sip of tea, wishing it was beer—preferably the potent local brew that tasted like battery acid and burned all the way down.

Quintin knew a lot of Ethan's history with Cassie. Early on, they had been snowed in for two days up here. After endless hands of poker and sharing a long fantasy about moving to some tropical island where it never got below sixty degrees, they had decided to drown their sorrows in cheap liquor. A lot of personal baggage had been unloaded.

Ethan gave his friend a sideways glance. "Why would you say an asinine thing like that? I just told you how the woman makes me crazy. She wants me out of her life so badly I can feel her boot heel on the back of my jeans."

"Maybe not."

"There's only one direction for this relationship to

go," Ethan said, tipping his chair forward with a thud. "Down."

Quintin, who, according to his own description, was half Arapaho and half mongrel, crossed his arms and shook his head.

"What?" Ethan said around the edge of his glass. "What's with the cigar-store Indian treatment?"

"'Methinks he doth protest too much.'"

"Learn that at your crappy reservation school, did you?"

"University of Arizona, kemosabe."

It was almost impossible to get under Quintin's skin or know what he was thinking. They relapsed into warm, golden silence. In the distance, Ethan could see Pikes Peak, still covered with snow from the heavy winter.

"What does she look like now?" Quintin asked unexpectedly.

He released a loud sigh. "Nearly the same, damn it," he admitted. "Still beautiful. Her face is thinner. There's a toughness about her that wasn't there before, like she's taken on the world and won."

"In some ways, she probably has."

"She wants me to think she's running this show." Ethan ran a distracted hand through his hair. "Hell, maybe she is. If I so much as look at Donny wrong..."

"Mother Bear will claw you to pieces to protect her cub."

Resting his elbows on his knees, Ethan tried to summon up logic from the chaos in his mind. "The thing is...the whole time I was thinking that I wanted to wring her neck, I was noticing that her hair was just as red as it ever was. She has a little strawberry birthmark on her shoulder, and I could hardly take my eyes off it. I remember when I…"

He straightened, feeling like an ass. "Hell, Quint, I'm completely insane! How can I still be attracted to someone who thought I wasn't good enough for her? She probably doesn't think I'm fit to be part of Donny's life, either, biological father or not."

"What does Henry think?"

Ethan had just returned from downtown Colorado Springs. His friend and attorney, Henry Vale, had missed his kid's soccer game just to meet with Ethan on short notice.

"He thinks I'm being premature, for one thing. He seems to think the adults ought to sit down and decide what we can be comfortable with as far as custody and responsibility. Then we can meet with our attorneys to make it official with a judge."

"Sounds reasonable."

"But not very likely. You should have seen Mama Bear's face. What Cassie wants is for me to disappear."

"So what do you do now?"

"Since Henry doesn't handle family law, he's going to hook me up with someone he trusts. In the meantime, there's a lot of preliminary information I'll need to get. Hospital records. Adoption papers. Henry even suggested I get a DNA test to make sure the kid is mine."

"*Are* you sure he's yours?"

"One look at him and you'd see the resemblance, Quint. Besides, I know Cassie. At least, the way she was back then. If she says he is, then he is."

"Still, it couldn't hurt."

"No, she wasn't the type to sleep around. And there's

no reason to put her through that, as if I don't trust her."

"You sound awfully protective of a woman you might have to fight in court."

Ethan swung his head to pin Quintin with a sharp look. A deep laugh lay at the bottom of the man's black eyes. For the first time since he'd returned from his meeting with Henry, Ethan felt his lips go into something like a smile. "Don't mess with me, pal. I'm in the mood to break something."

Quintin laughed, then rose to stretch. His rodeo days might be behind him, but the aches and pains still showed up occasionally. "So where does this leave our plans for Horse Sense?" he asked, after he'd worked the kinks out of his shoulders.

"There's no reason any of that has to change. Can you still trailer the horses down on Tuesday, along with the props?"

"No reason why not."

"Good. Assuming that Cassie isn't going to refuse to sell me the land, I should have the closing and building contracts nearly settled by the time you get there. I want to get a base camp set up by the end of April."

"That doesn't leave much time."

"All the better. Until I hear from Henry, I need to stay busy."

"Think you'll see the kid again?"

"I intend to."

His friend eyed him closely. "What exactly do you want here, Ethan?"

"I honestly don't know." He'd spent hours trying to come up with an answer to that. "Having a kid isn't anything I would have imagined for myself at this point in my life, but he's here, and I'm his father. I have to do what's right. I just wish I knew what that was."

CHAPTER SIX

WHEN THE FRONT DOORBELL rang a little after seven, Cassie knew it was Ethan. She wished suddenly that she could ignore it, that she could hide somewhere and refuse to come out. But that was silly, of course. After all, it had been her idea to invite him to dinner tonight.

She and Josh were prepared. Tonight they were determined to show Ethan the Wheeler family dynamic.

Donny had been told they'd have a guest, a friend from long ago and someone who intended to buy the property they'd been trying to sell for months. They'd asked him to be on his best behavior, but as was the norm lately, they couldn't be sure he'd gotten the message. It didn't help that just that day Donny had had a disagreement with his best friend, Russ. His mood could have been better, but what choice did they have but to proceed?

Cassie's best meal was ready for the table, and she'd even bothered to wear a pretty blouse with her jeans. Nothing clingy or fancy, just some soft, flowing spring thing in pale greens.

Donny was still upstairs. Josh gave her an encouraging look as she glanced back at him from the door. "Here we go," she said.

She smiled at him, wishing she hadn't spent the entire

day relying on her reserve of nervous energy, which was just about depleted by now.

She flung open the door.

She wasn't prepared for how handsome Ethan looked under the porch light. The suit he'd worn that first day had thrown her. But now, thirteen years began to melt away just like that. He was exactly the way she had always remembered him. Jeans and an open-necked Western shirt that revealed strong shoulders. His hair looked soft and slightly tumbled, no longer business-slick.

Every inch of him was designed to steal a woman's breath, and Cassie's defenses flared immediately. "You're late," she told him briskly.

He offered a fake smile and held out a bottle of wine. "Good evening to you, too."

She grimaced. This wasn't the way she wanted to start things. She realized that she was being sharp so as not to be afraid. "Sorry," she murmured. "Let me start over. Please come in."

"What did you tell Donny about my being here tonight?" Ethan asked softly as she took the wine from his hand.

"I just told him you were an old friend from the past."

He grinned, that devastating twist of his lips that had left her sleepless more than one night. "I suppose that's as close enough to the truth as we dare get right now."

He seemed more relaxed tonight, and here she was, buzzing with tiredness and tension.

Luckily, Josh entered the foyer just then. "Hello, Ethan. We're glad you could come. Would you like a drink?"

With the three of them on their best behavior, the social requirements of the evening got done. Had any discussion of the local weather ever been so thorough? There seemed to be a great deal of conversation between the men about inconsequential things, but Cassie supposed that was better than the two of them squaring off and pawing the ground, ready to go head-to-head. It all seemed very civil, very pleasant, and it made Cassie wince.

Finally, when Donny came down, he was reintroduced to Ethan, and Cassie quickly pushed everyone toward the dining room.

Trouble came almost immediately.

Josh and Cassie carried food to the table. As she slid a platter in front of him, Donny looked at it as if he'd been offered roadkill.

"What's *that?*" he asked. He sounded incredulous.

Oh, no, she thought. *Please.* "What do you mean? It's pot roast. Your favorite."

"I hate pot roast."

"Since when?"

"Since yesterday, when I told you I was gonna become a vegetarian."

This was the same boy who last week had said he wanted to be a mountain climber, who had given up golf after two lessons, and had once claimed he was going to sail around the world when he turned eighteen in spite of the fact that he got seasick in a canoe.

"I didn't realize you were serious," Cassie said between clenched teeth.

"Well, I was."

She plopped a bowl of vegetables in front of him. "So eat the carrots and potatoes."

"And that's all?"

Ethan, who was seated beside Donny and across from Cassie, spoke up. "I've heard a vegetarian lifestyle can be very healthy for you."

Josh laughed as he cut off a slice of beef. "Not in a cattle state like Texas, it's not. It's likely to get you kicked all the way to California."

Frustrated, Cassie said to her son, "You can become a vegetarian tomorrow. We can pick out some menus together. Tonight we're eating pot roast."

Donny grimaced, clearly unhappy. "Can I take a plate to my room?"

"*May* I. And no, you may not."

With a heavy sigh, Donny let Josh fork a slice of roast onto his plate. A moment later, he popped a bite into his mouth as though he had no objection at all.

Cassie glanced at Ethan. There was a glitter of amusement in his eyes. She gave him a pained smile and concentrated on unfolding her napkin.

They settled into the meal. With the exception of Donny, the men were complimentary about the roast, and the wine Ethan had brought went well with it. The ponderous weight of the unknown future floated around the table, but none of the adults were willing to acknowledge it.

Over the course of married life, she and Josh had had numerous friends over for dinner and, to an outsider, this might have been one of those times. Everything was exactly as it ought to be, and yet Cassie was perishing from something like panic. How could she sit here calmly, discussing the Dallas Cowboys, when Ethan sat across from her, making who knew what kind of plans for her son's future?

She glanced at Donny and realized right away that he was texting under the table. As though aware he'd been caught, her son met her stare.

"Put that away," she said quietly.

"I'm almost done."

"Now. And stop feeding Ziggy under the table."

"*He* likes your pot roast."

"I'm flattered, but stop feeding him. Zig, go lie down."

The dog obeyed, and Cassie was relieved when Donny did, too. She took another sip of wine, then frowned. *Whoa, girl.* She could see the bottom of her glass already.

"So where's your home now, Ethan?" she heard Josh ask.

She switched her attention to their guest. Big mistake. Ethan's eyes had found the light and gave it back. They were like blue windows full of warmth.

"I have twenty acres outside Colorado Springs," he said. "But I intend to build a place here, where I can spend half my time."

There was a long moment of dead silence. Cassie and Josh exchanged a look. Neither of them had expected to hear that Ethan intended to live on the land he wanted to purchase from them. They'd already signed the contract. If they refused to sell it to him now, they could be sued, but having him become their nearest neighbor half the year was not what they wanted to hear.

"Because of your business plans?" Josh finally asked.

Ethan's gaze connected with Cassie's for a moment before slipping back to Josh. "That's one reason."

Cassie straightened her spine, angling for defiance in

case he thought he could rattle her. Luckily, Josh kept the conversation rolling. "What are you going to do with that land?"

Ethan took another sip from his water glass. "My company needs to grow. In the past, Horse Sense has basically been a clinic for young or inexperienced riders who need help with their mounts."

"Like riding lessons?" Donny interjected around a mouthful of roasted potato.

"Not exactly. We deal more with horses that have behavioral issues. Things that frighten them. Loud noises, things popping up unexpectedly in front of them, suspicious obstacles that make them want to tear off in the opposite direction. We try to overcome their fear."

Cassie, who had realized she'd been staring too intently at his lips, caught his attention. "We?"

"I have a partner."

Donny swung his head to look at Ethan directly. It was the first time he'd actually bothered to take a real interest in the conversation or the man sitting beside him. "So what are you?" he asked. "Some kind of horse whisperer or something?"

"Nothing so mystical," Ethan replied with a short laugh. "Although Quintin, my partner, is part Arapaho, and I swear he can communicate with horses in a way I can't."

Josh spread butter across another roll. "Then you intend to hold clinics on that land? I wouldn't think Beaumont would offer enough business."

"It won't, but it's a good central location for this region. And we're planning to refocus our program. I've got a contract with the National Mounted Police Association to train their men and mounts to work together.

They need a standardized course, and someone who can weed out the stock that can't cut it."

"So we'll have cops everywhere in town?" Donny asked with a gleam in his eye. "Guess I'd better stop smoking weed behind the gym."

"Donny!" Cassie exclaimed, cringing inwardly. She stiffened as she glanced at Ethan. "He's joking."

"Whatever you say, Mom." Donny laughed, and she could have throttled him. Ethan had to know the boy was kidding, right?

To her relief, Ethan just smiled, as though he understood Donny's behavior perfectly.

"What made you want to do that?" Donny continued. "Teaching horses to chill out."

Ethan gave his son his full attention. "Over the years I've had...friends who've been seriously hurt by frightened horses. I wanted to see if I could prevent that."

"Mom got bunged up by a horse when she was young," her son said, then glanced toward her. "Didn't you, Mom?" His gaze bounced back to Ethan. "You ought to see her cool scars. Did you know her before that happened?"

"Yes." Ethan's gaze moved back to Cassie. "I remember that accident. But your mother was always a survivor who never let anything keep her down for long."

She took a breath, trying to find her equilibrium. She couldn't afford to be beguiled by this man. The fluttering sensation spreading outward from her abdomen needed to be stopped in its tracks. And yet the only thing that would form in her mouth was a polite, "Thank you."

Josh must have sensed her discomfort. He asked for more green beans. Then, in an obvious effort to change the subject, he motioned toward Cassie. "Cassandra's got big plans for that money from the sale. Tell him, honey."

"The Flying M has always run cattle. That's always paid the bills. But in the past few years, I've been trying to build a respectable breeding pool for Arabians. I'd like the ranch to become the premier place in Texas to find Arabs."

Ethan's brow lifted. "I'm surprised. I remember your father thought Arabs were too temperamental, too delicate. Nothing but a quarter horse would suit him."

"True," she admitted. "But I think he would be pleased with the changes I'm trying to make here."

"If I recall, he wasn't an easy man to please. But if that's your plan…" Ethan lifted his wineglass. "Good luck to you. I don't doubt that you can do anything you set your mind to."

"Thank you," she said again. "I think I can."

There were a few moments of silence while everyone except Donny seemed fixated on their food.

Eventually, her son turned toward Ethan again. "When you get all set up, can I come over to watch you work?"

"That would be up to your folks."

Cassie felt her heart miss a few beats, this time with fear. The last thing she wanted was for Donny to spend any real time with Ethan. Alone. "We'll see," she replied noncommittally.

"That means no," the boy stated sullenly.

"It means we'll see," Cassie said. "I'd much rather have you here studying to get your grades up than over there bothering Ethan."

"I'm sure he wouldn't be a bother," Ethan said.

She refused to look at him. Once again an uncomfortable silence descended.

Josh changed the subject, nudging Donny's arm. "Have you talked to Russ lately?"

"Yeah."

"How is he?"

"Fine."

"Have you two decided between the Rocky Mountains or the Bahamas?"

"No."

In the face of such monosyllabic rudeness, Josh turned to Ethan. "Every year, as soon as school lets out, the three of us go on vacation with another couple who have a son Donny's age," he explained. "We've been doing it since the boys were in kindergarten. This year we thought we'd leave it up to them whether to go white-water rafting in the Rockies or to the beach on a cruise." He glanced back at Donny. "I'll bet you and Russ can hardly talk about anything else."

Cassie suspected Josh had brought up the subject as a way of showing Ethan what a real family they were. But she'd forgotten to tell him about the fight, and from Donny's surly expression this was clearly the wrong topic.

"Why would we talk about it?" Donny asked at last. "We're not going, are we?"

Josh looked genuinely surprised. "Why wouldn't we?"

"Because…you know…*the divorce.*"

"I know that can make it difficult sometimes, but why should that stop us? We didn't divorce the Stanleys. They're still our friends, Donny."

"How was I supposed to know that?" he complained

in an abrupt tone. "Divorced people don't hang around together. Wes Lonegan's parents don't even talk to each other anymore."

"We're not Wes Lonegan's parents," Cassie cut in, wishing she could diffuse this situation, but knowing she was completely powerless to do so. Across from her, she was aware of Ethan listening, revealing not a single thought.

"Your mother and I are still good friends, son," Josh said calmly. "I'm sitting right here." He placed his hand along Donny's arm. "That's hardly not talking."

Donny shook off his father's hand and stood so suddenly that his chair slid back with a screech. His face was beet-red. "Fine! You two work it out however you want. Then maybe you can text me, 'cause no one around here bothers to tell me anything!"

"Donny!" Josh said loudly.

The boy ran from the table and pounded up the stairs. A few moments later, they heard the sound of his door slamming with a loud bang.

The atmosphere in the dining room went flat and tense so quickly that Cassie could hear the grandfather clock ticking in the foyer. Her breathing seemed so tight she felt light-headed. Josh's jaw was set like iron. Across from her, Ethan seemed preoccupied, playing with his knife.

Josh stood. "I'll talk to him."

When he had left the room, Cassie rose as well and began gathering dishes. "He's not usually like that," she explained. "As I told you, he's going through a tough time right now."

Ethan didn't respond. Didn't even look at her.

Feeling sick, Cassie headed for the kitchen with a handful of dirty dishes.

She placed them gently in the sink and ran water over them. She felt grief-stricken. She had wanted the evening to go well. It seemed imperative that Ethan come away from this dinner with the impression that his son was part of a happy, loving family—in spite of the divorce. A family that could hold up just fine without his involvement. What must he think now?

Tears clogged her throat. To calm herself, she pushed away from the sink and sat down on one of the kitchen stools. Her legs felt rubbery, and as usual, her left calf ached from the workout she'd given it today.

She closed her eyes, absently rubbing her hand down her jeans to ease the pain. Was there any way to salvage the evening? What could she do now?

"Are you all right?" a soft voice asked, and she opened her eyes to find that Ethan had joined her. He looked solemn. Cassie could guess his thoughts as clearly as if an artist had drawn them.

She stood, putting on the best face she could. "Yes, I'm fine. It's just a cramp." She made a move to go around him. "I'll get dessert."

He stopped her with a hand on her arm. "Let me help."

"That's not necessary."

He pushed her back onto the stool. "Sit down."

She thought he meant to get the peach cobbler off the counter, but instead, he drew up another stool and sat. Before she realized his intentions, he had lifted her bad leg, positioned it across his thigh and placed his hand on her knee.

He glanced up at her. "I don't want to hurt you, so tell me if I do, and I'll stop."

She was stunned. "Stop."

"I've barely touched you."

"That doesn't matter. This isn't appropriate."

He'd begun running his hands down her calf, squeezing, massaging. It felt very strange, but oddly wonderful. "Considering the circumstances," he said, "how much more inappropriate can I be?"

He seemed completely absorbed in helping her, and she began to tingle at the feel of his fingers working magic. Even though she was quaking inside, she also felt as though she wanted to close her mind down, give it a rest. It had been such a long, tense day. So much to think about. And worry over. What she wouldn't give to let someone else carry this burden of stress for a little while.

"You have very strong hands."

"I've rubbed down many a gimpy nag in my time." He lifted his head, giving her one of those impossibly sexy grins. "Oops, sorry. Didn't mean to sound like I was comparing you to a horse."

She had to smile back. He was being so nice, so considerate. But he was such a threat to her happiness. Why couldn't she just hate him and be done with it? It would have made everything so much easier.

"Is that any better?" he asked after a while.

She made a sound that was low down inside her, all hurt, nothing else. Unexpectedly, she watched a tear splash against his hand.

He looked up quickly, frowning. When he saw her face, he straightened on the stool. "Cass...damn, I'm sorry. Why didn't you say something if I was hurting you?"

She shook her head. She hadn't even realized she'd been crying until that tear had fallen. Now she knew that her cheeks were wet with them. They felt blazing hot, too, and she lifted her hands to wipe them away.

"It's not that. It's just that I wanted tonight…" The courage seemed bled out of her, but how could she tell him how she really felt? The fear. The worry. For all intents and purposes, this man had the power to turn her life upside down.

"It's nothing," she said at last.

"Yeah," he replied. His hand came out, and he caught one of her tears against his finger. "I can see that."

She could only stare at him, the quiet hum of the refrigerator the single sound in the room. Her mind raced, searching for an explanation, waiting for the tightness in her throat to relax.

In the end, she didn't have to say anything.

He unfurled a smile even as his forehead puckered. "Do you really believe I'm some sort of monster?" he asked. His voice, with its smooth texture and husky undertone, made her stomach take flight against her will.

"I don't know what to believe about you," she admitted. "It's been so long."

He shook his head. "Sometimes it doesn't feel like even one day has gone by." Before she could stop him, his hand slid against the side of her face like warm silk, fingering a curl. "Look, I realize I want something from you that you're not willing to give right now, but I'm not here to judge or find fault with the job you and Josh have done."

"He's a great kid. It's just that he's…he's…"

"Like we were at that age?"

"Maybe you," she said, feeling better for the first time since he'd come into the kitchen. "I was always Daddy's obedient princess."

"Until I came along," he added with an amused quirk of his lips. And then, for just a second, their thoughts seemed to mesh and there was a vibration between them, something like regret, unbearably sad.

Finally, with a sigh, Ethan moved away from her. His features were tamed once more. "It's true that I came here tonight with a specific agenda. I was determined to make my intentions clear to you and Josh. But I can see this isn't the time."

His words were a lifeline, and she grabbed it. "What are you saying?"

"You said Donny knows Josh adopted him?"

"Yes. We told him about a year ago."

"What have you told him about his real father?"

She could hardly look at him now. "Very little, actually. I told him his father was a good man, but that we just weren't suited for one another. Donny didn't press."

Ethan snorted and shook his head. "I guess this is where it *gets* pressed, then. I want Donny in my life, Cassie. I want him to know his father. But I can see that you have insecurity issues with him that need to be dealt with first. I don't know how you do that, and I don't know how long it will take, but I'm willing to wait." He gave her a look full of resolve, but understanding, as well. "At least for a little while."

CHAPTER SEVEN

A LITTLE OVER A WEEK later, Ethan and Quintin were
working in the meadow side by side, trying to lay out
the perimeter of a small corral where horses would be
worked on lunge lines. It was boring, hot work, and
Ethan found his mind wandering.

He had stayed away from the Flying M. He didn't see
Donny at all. True to her word, Meredith Summerlin had
pushed through the paperwork for the sale of the land,
so he'd seen Cassie with Josh at the closing yesterday.
She'd seemed preoccupied and unwilling to engage in
more than the most basic of pleasantries. They did not
discuss his son.

In a way, it was a good thing that they had so little
interaction.

He had always been a man who made decisions
quickly. He liked to get things done and settled. Though
he'd tried to work on it over the years, he wasn't known
to have a great deal of patience.

Once he'd returned to Beaumont after meeting with
his attorney, he'd been ready for answers, eager to put
plans in motion. Most of all, he'd wanted to get to know
Donny better.

But the night he'd had dinner at the Flying M had
shown him the unlikelihood of quick fixes. Donny's
behavior had made it obvious there were still problems

that Cassie and Josh had to deal with as they struggled to help the boy adjust to their divorce.

He didn't seem like a bad kid, in many ways, he was just a typical teenager. But something this delicate couldn't be coerced into happening overnight. There was no point in making things worse for the boy by forcing him to accept another big change in his life.

Ethan knew his best bet was to rely on Cassie's judgment, but that thought grated him. If he allowed her to call the shots and set the pace, it was possible this situation could stretch out indefinitely. And it seemed unlikely that she'd be singing his praises during that time. In spite of her claims otherwise, Ethan didn't think she'd looked all that hard for him thirteen years ago.

But what choice did he have? She knew Donny best. And if there was one thing Ethan had taken away from that dinner with the Wheelers, it was that Cassie loved their son completely.

So time it was, damn it. And patience. And distractions were the order of business in the meanwhile.

There were plenty of those, Ethan knew. He had his hands full. The Jackalope property was his, and the contractors he'd hired would be ready to start in two days. Quintin had come down with the horse trailer and a truckload of equipment they'd need for an obstacle course. The first clinic was scheduled for mid-June, and the end of April was still a week away.

Ethan went to bed every night in his hotel room buzzing with exhaustion and achy from a day spent dealing with a dozen different challenges, a hundred tiny irritations. A schedule like his should have had him snoozing within ten minutes.

Instead, he often found himself tossing and turning,

glancing at the Halloween-green glow of numbers on his bedside clock over and over again. He just couldn't sleep. And the reason was annoyingly obvious.

Cassie.

Sure, he wanted to see Donny again. He was eager to find out what else they had in common besides looks and a cocky attitude. But, though he hated to admit it, he wanted to see Cassie, too.

That night at dinner he'd been hard-pressed to keep his eyes off her. She'd looked so desirable in the soft light, her hair like dark autumn leaves, that frothy blouse so modest, and yet undeniably sexy.

He knew how hard she had tried to make the evening a success. He'd watched her shift uncomfortably every time the conversation stalled, watched her cringe whenever Donny misbehaved. Ethan had wanted to hug her, to take her in his arms and tell her it would be all right.

When he'd joined her in the kitchen and seen that she was almost in tears, he had wanted to do more than that. He'd wanted to do stupid things that made mincemeat of all logic and every bit of his common sense. He could not get the memory of her sweet, troubled face out of his head, the quaint and somehow heartrending dignity in her every movement.

It had taken all his powers of concentration to go no further than touch her cheek. Somehow he had found his way back to sanity, and to focusing on one goal. Donny.

But God help him, Ethan still couldn't resist her.

"You plan to take root there, partner?"

He swung around, realizing that he'd been daydreaming while Quintin waited for him to make a decision about the horses. They'd erected a primitive campsite on the property—tent, sleeping bags, cookstove—but had yet to rig up something for their mounts that would suffice until they finished building the corral and barn.

"Sorry," Ethan said. "Where were we?"

Quintin gave him an amused glance. "Well, *I* was suggesting we consider renting out temporary stall space for Houdini and Azza. I don't know where *you* were."

Ethan refused to rise to the bait. He knew he'd been preoccupied a lot lately, but he really didn't want to talk about it. Not even with a good friend like Quint. "Yeah, I think you're right," he acknowledged. "I don't mind if we have to rough it for a few weeks. We've put up with worse. But I'd like something better for them."

"Think our nearest neighbor has some extra stall space?"

The suggestion surprised him. "The Flying M? It probably does, but I don't know how willing they'll be to rent it out to us."

"To *you*, you mean. They don't even know me. If they did, they'd love me."

"Sure they would. That sparkling personality of yours gets 'em every time."

Quintin ignored the sarcasm, but something like mischief showed in his dark eyes. "Well, if you don't want to ask her, I could go over in a little while."

"Why you?"

"Guess I'd just like to meet the woman who can mess with your mind so thoroughly."

"*I'll* take care of it. I'll go after lunch."

"All right," Quintin said in obvious disappointment. "But be nice. Remember, this is something we want." He moved to one side suddenly, glancing over Ethan's shoulder. The entry road to the property was only three hundred feet away. "Looks like we have company."

Turning, Ethan saw a man approaching in the noon-day sun. With nothing more than a backpack on his back, he could have been a hiker, although his stride betrayed his age. Something about his stooped posture rang a bell for Ethan, but he didn't know why.

He stood under the trees, waiting for the stranger to reach them. When he did, when he stood directly in front of him, Ethan's pulse lurched.

"Hello, son," Hugh Rafferty said, breaking the long moment of silence between them. "You look surprised to see me."

Almost unconsciously, Ethan's fingers curled inward into fists, like a sweater that had been too tightly knit. He hadn't seen this bastard for years. No reason to. When he'd left home, Hugh Rafferty had disappeared from his life as easily as if he had drowned. His father had been an abusive, unfaithful husband, a drinker and a loser. Ethan had wanted nothing further to do with him. He still didn't.

His father grinned, showing a row of crooked teeth. "I'll bet you thought I'd be dead by now."

"I thought you might be."

"But here I am," the man said, dramatically spreading his hands wide. "Big as life."

The years had etched greater imperfections on his features. His cheeks were more hollow than Ethan re-membered, and there were more lines. His voice sounded grainy and tired, in spite of his smile, but Ethan refused to be moved.

"What do you want, Dad?" The question came out as

baldly as he intended, without the least bit of welcome or interest.

"It isn't what I want. It's what I can give. I'm here to help."

Another thick, awful silence. Ethan sensed Quintin move closer, almost protectively. "If everything's all right here, I think I'll check on the horses."

"Everything's fine," Ethan replied. He didn't need his friend to watch his back. He would deal with this himself, quickly. Firmly. When Quintin headed toward the horses and was out of earshot, he crossed his arms and stared down into his father's face. In the unforgiving sunlight, the older man looked pale, but still smiled as though they were the best of buddies. "What's this all about?"

"I don't blame you for being suspicious," Hugh said. "I suppose I taught you that—never trust anyone. I was a pretty lousy father, wasn't I?"

Ethan shifted uncomfortably. His patience was ebbing fast. "Look, I'm not interested in revisiting ancient history. I don't know how you found out where I was, but—"

"Actually, it took me almost two years to find you. I've been using the computer at the library every week, hoping your name would pop up somewhere, but you've kept a pretty low profile all these years. But two days ago, I saw the article they did about you and Horse Sense. When I realized you were within spitting distance, I put on my walking shoes. So here I am."

Last week, a local reporter had come out to the property and interviewed Ethan about the new business he intended to bring to Beaumont. Ethan had looked at it as great publicity, but if he'd known it would bring his father to his door, he'd have said hell no.

"I'm only going to ask you one more time," Ethan said. "Why are you here?"

"Told you. I want to help. I taught you nearly everything you know about horses, and I figure you can use an extra hand right now."

"I have a partner, and we're managing fine."

"Didn't you put an ad in the Beaumont paper looking for help?"

"Yes, but—"

"Just not my kind of help, right?" Hugh finished for him. He shook his head, as if talking to someone who didn't understand a thing. "I don't blame you for not welcoming me with open arms."

"Welcome you?" Ethan snapped, drawing himself up in tight control. "I don't want to have anything to do with you. The only question I have is why you aren't back home passed out on the couch after the usual weekend binge."

Hugh gave him another affable grin. "Can't. The bank took the couch and the house with it." He slapped a hand to his backpack strap. "Everything I own is right in here."

"So that's why. You need money."

"Nope. I need a job." For the first time since he'd shown up, Hugh suddenly gave him a serious look. "And I need to make things right with you."

Ethan's teeth clamped together. He would not respond to this. Whatever his father had in mind, it wasn't going to work. He stared at the man with cold speculation, refusing to speak.

Hugh grimaced. The skin around his mouth sagged

like melting wax. "I know what you're thinking," he said somberly, erasing the sly humor from his face. "But my liver mutinied on me, so I don't drink anymore. I don't carouse or cheat or chase women till I reek of cheap cologne. I'm a reformed man, son. I don't expect you to believe me, but it's true. Two years now." He held out one hand that was wrinkled and dense with liver spots. "Look at that. Steady as a rock."

"Good. Glad to hear it. But I'm not hiring yet. Cash is tight right now."

"Fine. I'll work for space in the tent and stale coffee. Wouldn't be the first time I've slept out under the stars."

"Don't you get it?" Ethan growled at last. Hostility toward his father had been carved deep into his soul years ago, and it wasn't going anywhere. "I don't want you here. I don't care if you're reformed. I don't care if you need to work through some twelve-step program to get right with the people you've hurt. I'm fine with things just the way they are between us. Now—"

Unexpectedly, his father reached out, grabbed his upper arm and gave it a shake. His grip was surprisingly strong. "Don't *you* get it? I'm not taking no for an answer. I've been searching for you for two years, and I'm not going away now. I can do most anything you throw my way, and from the looks of things here, some extra help would come in handy. So…" His eyes darted desperately, as if for inspiration. "So put me to work, or I'll hike back into town and tell the local fuzz that you robbed me of every cent I had."

"That's ridiculous. Do it. No one will believe you."

A hint of uneasiness crossed Hugh's face, but he

wiped it away instantly with another look of sheer resolve. "Doesn't matter. Once I make the claim, they'll have to investigate. You want to deal with a lot of unpleasant publicity, when what you need is to get this place up and running as soon as possible?"

"So you're a reformed man who believes in blackmailing people to get your way?"

Hugh didn't seem offended at all. "I'll do what I have to to make things right." He chewed his inside cheek for a long moment, then glanced down at his boots. When he looked at Ethan again, his eyes were shadowed and serious. "Please. I'm different. Give me a chance to prove it to you."

Ethan's nerves hummed. He didn't like the determined glint in his father's eyes, and he definitely didn't like that the firm *no* in his head had become vague and cloudy. His father never saw anything through. He'd get tired of doing grunt work and getting very little to show for it. In a day or two, he'd probably be on the road again, headed who knew where. That would be fine with Ethan. The sooner the better.

Feeling like a fool, he swung away from his father. "Quint!" he called to his partner. "Put this guy to work. Don't take any crap from him, and don't let him goof off. I'll be back this afternoon."

With a sense of complete unreality, he strode past Hugh Rafferty. His father said nothing, which was probably just as well, because Ethan couldn't have responded. His throat felt as though he'd swallowed a balloon.

What the hell was wrong with him? Letting that mongrel bastard back into his life for even an hour would be disastrous.

Ethan headed for his truck, and it wasn't until he'd pulled onto the paved road that he could even breathe again.

SEATED AT THE DESK in her study, Cassie glanced up from the spreadsheet on her computer to check the clock. She frowned. Another three hours before Donny got home. How the time seemed to drag on school days. While it was absolutely true he could be a downright pain in the neck sometimes, she missed him terribly when he wasn't around.

As though in sympathy, Ziggy came up and laid his head along her thigh. The border collie's huge dark eyes looked as miserable as Cassie felt. He was devoted to Donny.

"He'll be home soon," she told the old dog as she gave his ears a scratch. "Want to go for a walk?"

Ziggy perked up at those words and headed straight for the door, tail wagging. With a few keystrokes Cassie left her accounting program and shut down the computer. She hadn't been able to concentrate much on ranch figures, anyway.

Every day she became more and more concerned that Ethan might have reached the end of his patience. But a week had passed without incident since the night they'd invited him to dinner.

She'd furnished his attorney with some basic information about Donny, but there had been nothing since. No unnerving documents in the mail. No calls from either her lawyer or his. No Ethan.

Cassie's nerves felt as if they were being slowly shredded.

How clever of him. Finding a way to torment me without having to do a thing.

But even as she had that thought, she knew it wasn't true. Ethan had never been small or petty, and when he was angry with you, he let you know it. He didn't play cruel games. Of course, there had probably never been this much at stake before.

If he wanted Donny...

As she and Ziggy made their way to the front door, Cassie tried to imagine what it might be like to live in this house alone. No Josh. No Donny. A tomblike place stripped of laughter and joy.

You could convince yourself that loneliness and solitude were the ideal conditions, even a kind of freedom. But living here by herself was unthinkable. Even shared custody would be unbearable, though she knew thousands of parents came to such agreements every day. But if a judge thought she'd behaved outrageously, keeping a father in the dark about his son all these years, he might rule more favorably for Ethan. Then what?

All-out war between them? What would that do to their son?

She had to stop thinking about it. Instead, she reminded herself that Ethan had been fair and decent that night after dinner. In fact, his behavior, and her response to him, had only given her one more thing to worry about. How was it possible to be attracted to the one person in the world who had the potential to hurt you?

Maybe *attracted* was too strong a word. Once upon a time, perhaps... But that was long over, long behind the both of them. She couldn't help being *mildly interested* in him. His business venture here in Beaumont sounded intriguing. The stories he'd shared at the table about the years he'd passed after leaving Texas had been amusing, engaging. Probably for Donny's sake, but they made her want to know more. There was no reason to think—

Oh, who was she kidding? Ethan was still drop-dead sexy, and that night in the kitchen, when he had been so kind and understanding, she had realized that thirteen years of leading separate lives hadn't made one bit of difference. His touch on her leg had ignited a wanting in her that she hadn't experienced in ages.

It was all hormonal, she had assured herself. But she still couldn't stop thinking about it.

She spent a few minutes throwing a stick for Ziggy, until his tongue lolled and he refused to return it. She had barely entered the horse barn when she heard a vehicle pull up in the front driveway. Ziggy raced past her, barking as usual. Cassie followed more slowly, not eager for company, but suspecting it might be Josh, who had promised to stop by today. He planned to bring her a box of receipts he'd accidently taken over to River Bottom when he'd moved out.

She reached the entrance to the barn and saw that it wasn't Josh who had arrived. It was Ethan.

He came striding toward her purposefully, and something told her this wasn't a social call. Her heart stumbled a little. Had he decided that enough time had been wasted? Was he here to make threats and demands?

She refused to give in to anxiety, and decided to wait, to see what had brought him.

Her mouth forming a wary smile, she remained in the barn's doorway. When he reached her, she said quickly, "What's the matter?"

His forehead puckered. "Nothing. Why?"

"Because your face looks like a thundercloud."

"Sorry," he said with a grimace. "I have a lot on my mind lately."

She could imagine what that meant, but she wasn't willing to go there. Not yet. "How are things?" she asked instead. "The business, I mean."

"It's coming along."

"I heard some talk in town. People are excited."

"Good."

There was an explosion of fresh barking from Ziggy.

"Ziggy!" Cassie scolded. "Be quiet! Go chase something." As though he understood, the dog trotted back through the barn and out of sight. Cassie turned her attention to Ethan once more. "Sorry. You were saying?"

"I need to talk to you."

Ice settled into Cassie's backbone in spite of the warm April sunshine. Was this it? Was this the moment she'd been dreading all week? "About what?" she managed to ask.

"My partner has trailered our horses from Colorado. I'd like to rent stall space for them as soon as possible. Two, if you can spare them. With pasture access. Since you're my nearest neighbor…"

Cassie was filled with such relief she thought her knees might buckle. She gave Ethan a nod. "I'm sure we can arrange that. Come and see what we have."

She turned to head back into the barn, and Ethan fell into step beside her. The doors were open on both ends, letting in sunlight, but the place was still shadowed and cool. Many of the stalls had attached paddocks behind them, and from there, access to rich, green pasture. Ethan said nothing while he checked them out. There had been few changes since the time he had worked here.

When they reached the last stall, where the accident had happened, Ethan stared into it as though there were something special to see. Cassie rested her arms along the top railing, waiting.

"What happened to Bandera?" he asked in a low voice.

"Two days after the accident, Dad sold him. I was still in the hospital and couldn't do much to stop him."

Josh had told her that her father had loaded the stallion into a trailer bound for El Paso, then had gone inside the house where he got quietly drunk for the evening. As if the horse had ceased to exist, Bandera's name was never mentioned again.

Ethan expelled a sigh. "I'm sorry to hear it. Bandera wasn't really to blame for anything."

Such an awful, awful time for everyone, Cassie thought, as she stood quietly. How different things might have turned out if that accident hadn't happened. But it had, and there was nothing to be done for it now.

"Does it bother you to come here?" he asked.

"At first it did. But the barn didn't do anything wrong, either, and there was work to do. I couldn't allow this place to become haunted for me."

His eyes came to hers. The look in them was curious and uncritical, and it made her feel as if she were being suffocated by her heartbeats.

His gaze dropped to her leg. "You're limping. It hurts today, doesn't it?"

She gave him a conceding look. "A little. I've been sitting too long. An hour in the Torture Chamber will make everything better."

The words hung in the air, while Ethan seemed engrossed with picking a strand of hay apart. He glanced up at her. "I think you've become a very brave woman over the years," he said unexpectedly.

Time began to slide by, and to keep it from becoming uncomfortable, Cassie moved away from the stall, heading toward the back entrance of the barn.

Cochise, Donny's new horse, had been turned into the nearest paddock. The palomino trotted around the enclosure, head and ears pricked up, nostrils flared, as if he sensed something. He might be missing Donny. Or maybe was just annoyed by Ziggy's presence. The dog seemed determined to chase after the horse, barking encouragement.

"How are things going over here?" Ethan asked as he joined her at the fence.

"All right. We heard from your attorney. I've given him everything—birth records, adoption papers, medical history. I don't think I left anything out."

"So what's the holdup?"

His tone annoyed her. "You'll have to ask your lawyer. Ours has been instructed to cooperate. We're not stonewalling you, if that's what you're thinking."

"It occurred to me that you might."

She lifted her chin. "Then you really don't know me as well as you think. I can't pretend I'm happy about this situation, but I'm not going to run away from it, either. Be realistic, Ethan. It's only been a week."

"I'm used to fast results."

"Donny isn't a business plan that can be constructed. When we tell him about you, the time has to be right."

Ethan seemed mollified by her words, nodding slightly. "How is Donny?"

The question sent her mind into new, disturbing channels. She dreaded his interest, though it was only natural he'd ask.

"It depends on what day you're asking about," she replied, trying to sound as if she wasn't fracturing inside. "Monday Josh and I had a talk with him about what a friendly divorce can be like. I think he felt a little reassured. He finally admitted that all his friends told him divorced parents always start out trying to keep it pleasant for the sake of the kids, but it never ends up that way."

"That's a good sign, isn't it?"

She made a face. "Wednesday he skipped school to go to the movies and then lied to us about it. He has exams coming up, and he hates tests. We took away his TV privileges and he's still not speaking to us. Every day seems like a new challenge."

"I suppose you and Josh will figure it out."

"I suppose."

"You two intend to stay close. For Donny's sake."

She'd been watching Ziggy trot beside Cochise. Now she turned to look at Ethan, because those last words had been a statement, not a question. Something in his tone had changed. Some sort of tense challenge that hadn't been there before. "Of course we will."

"Any mention of me? From Donny, I mean."

"He's eager to see what you're creating over there."

"You know that's not what I mean."

"No. He hasn't mentioned you."

That comment seemed to irritate him, probably because he had hoped otherwise. It wasn't an entirely true response. Donny hadn't spoken of him in any real, personal way, but he had expressed an opinion. He thought Ethan had "juice." Cassie wasn't sure she understood what that meant, but the remark had annoyed Josh to no end.

Ethan plowed a hand through his hair. His jaw tightened. Along the edge of it lay a short, thin scar she'd never noticed before. A souvenir from his rough past, no doubt.

"I'm not going to wait forever, Cassie," he told her, his blue eyes harsh.

She lifted her chin. "I'm not asking you to."

"This doesn't have to get ugly between us."

"It will if your ultimate goal is to take Donny away from me. Away from Josh, who's the only father he's ever known."

She watched Ethan's hands on the fence. They gripped the wood so hard that his knuckles stood out, sharply white. She felt her stomach twist, knowing he was controlling his emotions, but just barely. "My ultimate goal," he said pointedly, "is to stop being excluded from my son's life."

She bit her lip, trying to keep her temper under wraps. The last thing she needed was to pick a fight. That would just make things worse between them. She started to say something, then rejected it. Finally, in frustration, she turned her face back toward the paddock as Cochise went running past them.

The horse seemed agitated, and right away, Cassie saw why. Ziggy, issuing occasional barks around a lolling tongue, playfully nipped at the palomino's heels. Donny's old horse hadn't minded these kind of games, but Cochise didn't seem to like it one bit.

"Zig!" Cassie called loudly. She was in no mood for this. "Come here!"

The wretched dog paid no attention. Just as Cassie

was about to enter the paddock and shoo him away, Cochise lashed out with a back hoof. He kicked Ziggy hard, and with a pained yip, the border collie dropped like a rock.

CHAPTER EIGHT

IN THE END, Cassie was thankful for Ethan's presence.

While she ran to Ziggy's side, he chased Cochise off to the far corner of the pasture, waving his arms while trying to settle the animal's nervous capering with his voice. When Cochise finally stood still, head lowered, snorting and blowing, Ethan came running back to Cassie.

He knelt beside her.

"Oh, you silly dog," she crooned to Ziggy, who was out cold. "What were you thinking?"

Ethan carefully lifted the border collie's head. It moved loosely on his neck, and when he withdrew his hand, his fingers were covered in blood.

"Oh, God," Cassie gasped.

"He needs a vet."

"Dr. Tyler is five miles from here."

"We have to stop the bleeding. Get a towel."

Cassie jumped up and ran to find one in the tack room. When she returned, Ethan twisted the cloth around the dog's head. Then he fished his keys out of his jeans pocket, dropping them into Cassie's palm. "Get my truck started."

Again she raced to follow his instructions. She glanced back and saw that he had lifted Ziggy in his arms and was gently carrying him toward the vehicle.

When it seemed as though he might lay the dog in the bed liner, Cassie caught his arm. "No. I want to hold him up front."

Quickly he placed Ziggy across her lap, then transferred his pressure hold on the towel to her. He jumped into the driver's seat, then swung out of the driveway. Cassie stroked the dog's fur with one hand and tried to keep a tight grip on the bloody towel with the other. Issuing directions to the vet's office, she braced herself as best she could when Ethan bounced onto the highway.

As they drove, she offered up every prayer she could think of. Ziggy might belong to Donny, but *she* was the one who took care of him most of the time. She loved him as much as her son did.

In Cassie's opinion, Leah Tyler was the best vet in the county. She'd been known to deliver a foal or two when the need called for it, but most of the time she stuck to domestic pets, and she'd been Ziggy's vet since he was a puppy.

As soon as Ethan came in with the bloody, unconscious dog in his arms, they were whisked back into one of the treatment rooms. Stretched out on the table, Ziggy looked so vulnerable. Cassie hated it when the vet technician placed a loose muzzle over his mouth.

The woman looked up at her. "It's just a precaution," she said. "In case he wakes up in a fighting mood."

If he wakes up, Cassie couldn't help thinking.

Ethan stood behind her. She felt his hand drop, warm and comforting, on her shoulder. "He'll be all right, Cass."

She nodded. "Yes, of course. He's just a very foolish dog, always getting into things he shouldn't."

Leah came into the room then. She was a pretty,

vivacious blonde, but she was all business when it came to treating animals. As Cassie explained what had happened, she examined Ziggy thoroughly. When they peeled off the towel, the blood had slowed to a trickle, but the wound was still a mess. After instructing her assistant to clean and shave the area, Dr. Tyler straightened. The look on her face frightened Cassie even more than the blood.

"He's an old dog, Cassandra," she said with a grimace. "And it looks like your horse got in one heck of a blow."

"But you can fix him."

"I hope so. I'll need to take X-rays. See if there's any fracturing or internal damage."

"Anything you need to do," Cassie said quickly. "How can I help?"

The doctor made a shooing movement with her hands. "Go. Let me do my job. I know you're worried, but if you stay here you'll only be in the way. I'll come get you as soon as I know something."

Cassie opened her mouth to protest, but never got the chance. Ethan was suddenly steering her toward the door. "Thanks, Doctor," he told the vet. "We'll be camped out in the waiting room."

He guided Cassie into the restroom, where she rinsed the blood off her hands and splashed cold water on her face. Then he cleaned up and came out to sit at her elbow. Surprisingly, there wasn't anyone else in the waiting room. The reception staff seemed busy with paperwork.

They waited. And waited. Forty-five minutes later there was still no word. It was awful, Cassie thought, the toll her ridiculous nervous system exacted in times of crisis. She bent forward, her loosened hair falling along her cheeks as she stared at the floor.

"It's taking too long," she muttered.

Ethan's hand rubbed her back. They hadn't spoken much since they'd sat down. His silence was broad and warm with sympathy, and he'd seemed to know instinctively that normal conversation would be impossible.

Not a breath of air stirred. It seemed unbearably hot in the waiting room, and yet a deep, gathering coldness of fear coiled within Cassie.

"I want to walk," she said, standing suddenly.

Ethan began to rise as well.

She pressed a hand against his shoulder. "No. I just need a minute. Some fresh air."

She rushed through the entrance door before he could say anything. She headed for the side of the building, then around the back. Behind the office was a sort of dog park, a place where the staff could exercise long-term care patients. A bench sat beside a tall, shady oak tree. She slid onto the seat, then closed her eyes.

It felt so good to sit here in the sweet, fresh afternoon air. She didn't want to go back to the claustrophobic waiting room, where bad news would surely find her.

Her eyes were still closed and she was letting the sunshine paint warmth along her lids when she heard movement. She lifted her lashes to see that Ethan had joined her on the bench.

He held out a water-cooled hand towel. "Sorry," he said with a grimace. "It's the only thing I could find on short notice. I'm not even sure why I think it will help."

She gave him a weak smile as she took it from him

and folded it behind her neck. "Thanks," she replied with a light groan of momentary pleasure. "It feels good."

"You're as white as a ghost."

"Can't help it. I'm scared. If Zig dies…" Unable to finish the thought, she let the implication lie there.

"I wish I could make this right for you, but I can't. You just have to trust Dr. Tyler to do her best."

"Suppose he's not okay? We've had him since Donny was a preschooler. If he dies, it will break my son's heart."

"He's not going to die."

"You don't know that." She flung the words back at him more sharply than she had intended. "I told Josh that Cochise was too much horse. We should sell him," she muttered, almost to herself. "Suppose it had been Donny that he kicked?"

"It wasn't."

Her heart reeled with possibilities. "Still, what if he's dangerous?"

"Let me work with him for you. And Donny, too."

"I don't know… Maybe another horse…"

Ethan's arm rested on the back of the bench. He brought his fingers up to rub her shoulders. Her heart reeled with the gentleness of his touch, even while the healthy instincts of self-preservation told her to pull away.

"Let me try," he coaxed softly. "I'm actually pretty good at this sort of thing. If the horse is a danger, I'll know it."

"Cassandra?"

They both turned to see Leah Tyler coming toward them. Cassie jumped up and away from Ethan's com-

forting hand. She hurried to join the vet, and Ethan
followed.

"How is he?" she asked, almost afraid to hear the
answer.

Dr. Tyler smiled. "I think he'll be fine. No skull frac-
ture. He lost quite a bit of blood, but it would have been
far worse if you hadn't put the pressure bandage on him.
I've stitched him up. He's not going to be pretty for a
while, but he'll be the old Ziggy before you know it."

"I hope not," Cassie said, barely able to keep relieved
laughter *and* tears at bay. "I hope he's learned his lesson.
Can he come home?"

"I'd like to keep him overnight. Just to be certain."

"Of course, sure. Can I see him?"

"For a minute. I'll take you in the back way."

Dr. Tyler turned and headed in the direction of the office's rear entrance. Cassie was so happy she was almost
breathless.

She turned toward Ethan. His smile wasn't quite as
wide as hers, but he looked equally pleased. "I can't
believe it!" she said in a voice filled with wonder. "He's
going to make it."

"Sounds like it."

Before she could stop herself, she threw her arms
around Ethan to give him a big hug. "Thank you!" she
told him, the words pouring out in joyful relief. "Thank
you for being there when I needed you."

She kissed him then. A quick, yet solid connection
that he clearly wasn't prepared for. The contact of his
lips against hers was warm and strong and helplessly
appealing, but when his arms began to come around
her, she pulled away.

"You're welcome," Ethan said. His grin wobbled somewhere between surprise and pleasure.

She stared at him, more than a little shocked herself. Just a thank-you kiss, that was all it was. Somehow, she couldn't find it in her heart to be sorry. Not in that moment.

She smiled back at him and fumbled for inspiration, some way to explain. Impossible. Without another word, Cassie turned and hurried after Leah Tyler.

BY THE TIME ETHAN HAD driven her back to the Flying M, Cassie was no longer operating on adrenaline. She felt bone-tired, drained, and the thoughts in her brain skipped around like a worn needle on an old record album.

That kiss. Had it really just been a thank-you? Or had she known what she was doing and been powerless to stop herself? Her father had always said that what was deep inside a person always surfaced, no matter how well hidden. But when it came to Ethan Rafferty, what *was* inside her? Aside from fear that he'd take her son away. The last time she'd looked, a person didn't go around kissing her enemy. Not even to say thank-you.

"Cass?"

She bumped back into reality, aware suddenly that Ethan had spoken. It surprised her to see they were in the Flying M's front drive, and that the truck engine was silent. She turned her head and found him watching her.

"I'm sorry," she said. "What were you saying?"

He turned toward her. "I asked if you wanted to talk about it."

"Oh, no," she replied, perfectly aware what he meant,

and perfectly determined not to go there. "I'm much better now that I know Ziggy will be all right."

"Nice try. But that's not what I was referring to."

"I have to go." She placed her hand against the latch, eager to escape. "Donny will be home from school soon, and I want to be prepared to give him the news."

Ethan caught her arm. "Cass, wait. There's time to talk."

"We don't need to talk," she told him as she swung back. Then she frowned. "I thought men were notorious for keeping things to themselves. You used to be the strong, silent type. Now suddenly you're Dr. Phil?"

He grinned. "You're really uncomfortable, aren't you? You kissed me, supposedly a simple thank-you kiss. Are you wondering if there was more to it than that?"

"No."

"That's okay, 'cause I'm wondering enough for the both of us. You can't stop thinking about it, and that scares the hell out of you, doesn't it?"

"I haven't been thinking anything…" she began to protest, then dropped that line of defense. Really, it was quite obvious what was wrong here. Even after all these years, she couldn't explain the spell Ethan cast over her any more than she could deny it, and they were both completely aware of that fact. Frustrated, she said, "The only thing that worries me is that I might have given you the wrong idea."

He leaned forward, shortening the distance between them until she could see devilish lights dancing in his eyes. "You want to try it again? See if you can give me the *right* idea?"

"Absolutely not. It was just an emotional moment—"

"I've been given thank-you kisses before. That wasn't one."

Her lips closed in what she was sure was a prim, straight line. "Well, I don't need this complication in my life right now." How thin and taut her voice sounded. "Or in Donny's," she added, forming the words carefully.

She pulled back on the door handle and got out quickly, relieved when Ethan made no move to stop her. Before slamming the door shut, she bent down to catch his eyes.

"Thank you for helping me deal with this today," she said, feeling that she still owed him a debt. But no more kisses. "You certainly didn't have to."

"I'm glad it turned out all right."

"Me, too."

He gave her a considering look, as though not certain he understood her anymore. "I'm not your enemy, Cassie."

"I'm not sure what you are," she told him. Then, before he could say anything, she closed the door and went up the front steps.

CHAPTER NINE

A SMALL CREEK RAN THROUGH the property Ethan had bought, and two days later, all he wanted to do was strip off his clothes and lie down in it to cool off.

The day had dawned hot and sticky, with very little breeze. Half the contractor's crew had called in sick, so construction moved at a crawl. Along with Quintin and Hugh, he'd been working all morning in the front meadow near the road, trying to maneuver some of the obstacle barricades and fake drop-walls into place. They hadn't made much headway, and none of them could pinpoint why.

Ethan supposed part of the problem was that he was unfocused and tired, which seemed odd since he was the only one still taking advantage of a hotel room at night. Quintin and his father preferred to camp out in the tent on the property. Ethan should have been able to claim a good night's sleep, but damned if a hot shower and a soft mattress made one bit of difference. He woke up barely rested, swaying with fatigue and as irritable as a grizzly.

If he had to list reasons for his restless lack of energy, he could choose three likely candidates.

First, his attorney had called to say that Cassie's lawyer hadn't been in touch. Right now, the Wheelers seemed to be ignoring requests for a formal meeting of all parties except Donny. Ethan thought he'd been pretty patient, but if they thought they could stonewall him and he'd go away, they were wrong.

Every so often, the urge hit him to climb into his truck and just show up at the ranch, demanding decisions. It was completely the wrong way to handle this, his lawyer had said, but it suited Ethan a lot more than this waiting game.

Second, there was Cassie. No use pretending he wasn't interested in seeing if their old relationship could be brought back to life. Cassie might be able to bury the memory of that kiss at the vet's, but he sure hadn't. He hadn't even wanted to.

It had been vivid. Intriguing. Such a short, insignificant kiss, but how sweet her lips had felt pressed against his. The heat of her body, warmed by the sun. Remembering every bit of it had been keeping him sleepless and horny as hell at night and leaving his bed looking like a war zone.

That hotel shower? Turned out he was as much in need of the *cold* water as he was the hot. Sometimes during the day—

"So, you ready to admit you're wrong?"

The three men had been working on one of the ramps that would lead to a water obstacle, and eventually knee-deep mud. No horse liked that. Hugh had returned to the campsite to retrieve a different wrench. Ethan straightened, realizing that Quintin had caught him daydreaming. "Wrong about what?"

His partner wiped sweat away from his brow with the sleeve of his shirt. "Your dad's a pretty sharp guy. I'm not sure you or I would have come up with his fix for that drop-wall problem."

Oh, yeah, reason number three Ethan was out of sorts lately. Hugh Rafferty. The old man was really insisting on earning his keep. "He's like a magician with a bag of tricks," Ethan said with a shrug. "He knows enough stuff to keep you wondering, but down deep, he's nothing but smoke and mirrors."

He glanced toward the camp tent. His father should have found that wrench and been back by now.

"Kind of tough on him, aren't you?" Quintin asked. "I've been right beside him every day for a week now, and I haven't seen anything but genuine hard work and a great attitude."

"You can't trust him. He'd pry the gold out of a dead man's teeth."

Quintin frowned. Ethan knew his tone sounded harsh, but his partner didn't know the man like he did. The fact that he'd been on his best behavior since showing up here was probably only to impress Ethan with how much he'd changed. But he couldn't go the long haul; sooner or later, he'd slip back to his old ways.

And whatever fledgling relationship they had—not much of one by anyone's standards—would be over. Just like that. One thing his father had always been an expert at—he knew how to make you hate him.

"You sure have turned suspicious since you've been down here," Quintin said.

Ethan tossed his hammer into one of the toolboxes and turned toward his partner. "With him it pays to be suspicious. He'll always disappoint you if you don't keep your guard up."

"If he's responsible for the skill you have with horses, he can't be all bad."

"He loves horses. It's people he has a problem with."

Ethan began striding toward the campsite. "I'll see what's keeping him."

As he approached the tent, he noticed that the front flap, usually open to allow fresh air to circulate, was closed. The tent was ideal for two men to camp comfortably, tall enough to stand up in and large enough for two cots, with room left over for storing duffel bags, ice chests and equipment.

With the backdrop of the morning sun, Ethan could see Hugh Rafferty's silhouette hunched over as he sat on his bunk. The thought flashed suddenly in Ethan's mind that maybe his father was sick. The morning heat had been pretty brutal.

Ethan threw back the tent flap so fast that Hugh jumped. Like a kid caught with his hand in the cookie jar, he looked up guiltily. "Boy!" he scolded, in the harshest tone Ethan had heard him use since showing up. "Scare the life out of me, why don't you?"

But the only thing Ethan cared about was that something had, a moment ago, been fisted in his father's hand. Whatever it was, Hugh had shoved it under his cot mattress because he clearly hadn't wanted Ethan to see it.

Anger pumped through him.

Stashing booze. Had to be. Maybe nothing bigger than an airliner's minibottle of Scotch, but something he didn't want anyone to see. Ethan remembered this kind of animal secretiveness from his father in the old days, back when he still cared who caught him.

Drunken bastard. Did he really think he could fool a son who had grown up watching him fall into a bottle nearly every night? The only amazing thing about this was that someone would believe a tiger could change his stripes. But that, Ethan thought with self-disgust, was exactly what had happened. He'd gone way beyond his better judgment with this man, and right on into stupidity.

There wasn't a single breath of air in the tent, but Ethan ignored the heat and stared down at his father. "Quintin and I are still waiting for that wrench."

"Sorry," Hugh said, his voice filled with contrition. "I haven't found it yet."

"This one?" Ethan asked as he leaned down to pick up the wrench from the toolbox at the bottom of Quintin's cot. He knew his voice was sharp, but he didn't care.

"Oh. Look at that. Right under my nose. Guess the old eyesight is going."

"Guess so."

Hugh grabbed the wrench, then jumped up, heading outside. When he realized Ethan wasn't right behind him, he turned. "You coming?"

Ethan shook his head. The outrage of betrayal was so thick in his throat he could barely speak. "I'll be along. I want to grab my gloves."

His father smiled at him. Ethan hated that smile; there was nothing behind it but corruption and lies. "See you in a minute, then," Hugh said, and left the tent.

When Ethan was certain the older man was well away, he went back to his father's cot. Lifting the thin mattress, he ran his hand underneath, certain it wouldn't be long before he encountered a bottle, maybe even more than one. He frowned when the only thing he came up with was a folded piece of paper.

He sat down on the cot and didn't hesitate to open the page of what appeared to be stationery. Whatever this was, it was clear his father hadn't intended for him to see it. Well and good for someone whom Ethan trusted to keep secrets from him, but the simple fact was, he had no faith that Hugh didn't have something up his sleeve. The commitment Ethan owed to the business and the obligation he had to Quintin made it easy for him to read whatever his father had been trying to hide from him.

The letter was written in splotchy ink, in a feminine hand. His eyes jumped to the bottom to see that it was signed by someone named Jean.

Dear Hugh,
Let me get right to the point. I've no doubt that AA can help a person atone for past mistakes, but after the way you treated my sister, after the life of misery you gave her, how could you ever expect me to forgive you?

Ethan stopped reading immediately. He'd almost forgotten that his mother had a sister named Jean, living somewhere on the West Coast—a small, spinsterish woman who'd hated his father nearly as much as he did. Obviously, this was the same person, and Hugh had made some previous effort to reach out to her, just as he'd shown up here. This letter was dated just last week. Evidently Aunt Jean wasn't having any part of his father's attempt to make amends.

Smart old biddy, Ethan thought as he folded and replaced the letter exactly as he'd found it. *Don't trust him for a minute.*

The only thing was, since his father had reappeared in his life Ethan couldn't honestly say that he'd done anything wrong. Quint had a point. Hugh had shown himself to be a dependable, steady, hard worker. He hadn't whined about a single chore. He kept quiet most of the time, and as soon as Ethan cut him off when he brought up the past, he shut up. He hadn't asked for money, stayed out all night or shown up drunk.

What *was* his father after, then?

Could it really be like the older man had said the day he'd shown up? He just wanted to be forgiven? Sober, ready to atone?

Oh, hell, that was the stuff of Hallmark movies, wasn't it? That was *not* Hugh "Riff-Raff" Rafferty.

Puzzled and more than a little frustrated, Ethan found his gloves and swept out of the tent, heading back to the water obstacle, where the other two men waited. He wanted to pretend that nothing had happened, that everything was the same as it had been ten minutes before, but he wasn't sure he could pull it off.

Every day, Hugh Rafferty continued to surprise him.

BY MIDAFTERNOON, the men had whipped the problems on the water obstacle into shape. Seated on logs positioned around the dead campfire, they were celebrating with massive bags of potato chips and washing them down with a gallon of sweet Southern iced tea.

"I knew we could do it," Hugh crowed as he shook a cluster of chips into his hand. "Just took the three of us putting our heads together."

Quintin snorted. "Take some credit, man. You're the one who solved the problem." He cut a glance Ethan's way. "Don't you agree?"

Ethan gave his partner a warning look, knowing what he was trying to do. Since Hugh had shown up, Quintin seemed determined to make peace between the two men, an idea Ethan had told him to forget. But Quintin could be stubborn, and when he set his mind to something, he wasn't subtle.

"Dad's always been creative," Ethan replied in an offhand way. For some reason he couldn't fathom, he felt compelled to add, "I appreciate the help."

Hugh looked surprised at this faint praise. Unable to meet his eyes, Ethan took a large swallow of tea so that he wouldn't have to do any more talking.

"Wonder what our visitor thinks of all this," his father said, lifting his chin toward the pine woods that bordered the property, about a hundred yards away.

Ethan turned and caught a glimpse of movement among the trees. A horse and rider, doing their best to be inconspicuous. Donny's palomino munched grass while its owner sat cross-legged on the ground.

"Anyone know who that is?" Hugh asked. "He's been sitting out there for over an hour."

Ethan stood, depositing his chips and drink on the top of an ice chest. "Neighbor kid. His name's Donny. He's just curious to see what we're doing."

He headed off in the direction of the woods. He hadn't seen Donny since that night at dinner, and he was glad to have this opportunity present itself. Any time spent together out from under the watchful eyes of Cassie or Josh was a plus.

As he moved closer, Donny jumped up, as if he intended to ride away. "We've seen you," Ethan called to him. "Might as well stick around."

The boy waited for Ethan to approach. He stiffened to make himself look taller, more adult, but his hands betrayed him. His fingers twisted the reins, as though he expected a lecture.

"I didn't do anything wrong."

"I didn't say you did."

"Mom said I wasn't to bother you, but I just wanted to see what you guys are up to. It looks like you're building a haunted house."

Ethan glanced back at the meadow, where they had constructed the skeleton of a couple of rooms, one with waving sheets for walls, the other with low-hanging leather straps swaying from the overhead beams. He nodded. "In a way, we are. As we pull certain levers, those sheets and straps will flap back and forth. When a horse is ridden past, it will be terrified to be touched unexpectedly. We're going to teach its owner how to overcome that."

Interest gleamed in Donny's eyes. "I get it. Like you said the other night. Cochise wouldn't be scared, but my old horse would sh—" He took half a breath, rethinking. "My old horse wouldn't like it."

Ethan had to resist smiling. He had to admit he was a sucker for this kind of scruffy, wounded rogue. At that age, he hadn't been much different.

"Nope," he agreed. "Horses definitely don't like that sort of thing. Too many blind spots. But by the end of our class, it should be willing to walk through them without stopping." He pointed toward one corner, where mattresses lay on the ground like a carpet long enough for a coronation. "Same thing with the mattresses over there. Makes an animal feel unstable to walk over them, but they'll learn."

He explained in great detail what Horse Sense hoped to accomplish with the Mounted Police Association. As he had before, Donny asked great questions that Ethan barely had time to answer. His son's face was alive with intelligence and charm today. Somewhere inside, Ethan felt something squeeze tight. He almost always felt uncomfortable around children, but not this one, and it didn't have anything to do with the fact that Donny was his. Well, maybe a little. But how could you not enjoy a kid like this?

When Ethan finished, Donny stroked the side of his palomino's head. "I don't think Cochise needs that kind of schooling. He's really smart, and what he doesn't know…" He shrugged. "My dad says we can work on him together. He's really good with horses."

It took everything Ethan had in him not to react to that statement. This was *his* kid, damn it. He was the father who specialized in working with horses.

"Even the best horse can learn a few things," he said evenly. "Maybe we'll put Cochise through his paces one of these days."

"Cool." Donny eyed Ethan. "Mom said you were there when he kicked Ziggy. Can you get him to stop that?"

"Actually, I think I can. How *is* Ziggy, by the way?"

"Back to normal." The boy laughed. "Whatever that is. Mom babies him and won't let him out of her sight right now."

How easy it was for Ethan to picture Cassie crooning to that idiot dog, wrapping her arms around him, stroking his fur. Lucky beast. Worth a kick in the head to get that kind of interest from Cass. Ethan's mouth went dry and his brain tied itself up in knots the way it had for days now, every time he thought of her.

He had to clear his throat just to speak. "Your mom's very protective of all of you."

"I guess. But it sure is a pain in the neck sometimes, when everyone's telling you what to do all the time."

"Life's tough," Ethan couldn't resist commenting. "Sometimes you don't always get to do what you want." If ever there was a more rock-solid truth about life, he couldn't think of one.

Cochise, evidently growing impatient with all this standing around, nudged Donny's back a couple of times. Then he moved forward, as though he was ready to go even if his master wasn't. The horse was strong enough that he almost unbalanced the boy.

"Quit it, Cochise," Donny scolded, then said it again more forcefully when the animal didn't stop. "Knock it off! We're going soon enough."

"Your horse needs better ground manners. He should stand still until you tell him it's all right to move."

"He gets bored sometimes."

"He's a herd animal, and you're the lead broodmare. He's supposed to mind you."

Donny puffed out his chest playfully. "*Broodmare?* No way! I'm the alpha stallion."

"Sorry," Ethan replied with a shake of his head. "The stallion fights off danger, but the top mare leads the herd away to keep them safe. Everyone else does what she says because she's the one who can really protect them."

"Just like girls, huh? Always trying to run the show."

Ethan didn't know how to respond to that, so he just grinned.

"Okay," Donny said in an amused tone as he held out Cochise's reins. "Can you show me how to be the lead broodmare?"

Ethan took the leather lines. "Come with me," he said, and both Cochise and his son followed as he turned and headed back to camp.

Over the next hour, Ethan put Donny and the palomino through his usual course assessment tests. The kid had a surprisingly mature seat, strong muscle control in his legs and good coordination. He had a tendency to give Cochise too much freedom in the bit and didn't work his neck enough, but he handled the animal confidently. He wasn't afraid of his horse's massive power and what it could do.

Next, Quintin came over to help, while Hugh and Donny watched. Ethan snatched up a long lead to lunge Cochise in the round pen they'd constructed. Every time the animal refused to remain still after a verbal command of "Stand," he lunged him again, until the horse broke into a hard sweat.

"He's getting tired," Donny said, throwing the men a worried glance.

"That's the idea," Hugh told him. "Horses are lazy cusses by nature, and he's got to learn that if he's not going to get with the program, he'll have to work."

Finally, Ethan joined them at the fence, leading a snorting, wet Cochise behind him. "A few more sessions like that," he told Donny, "and he'll get the message. Think you can keep up the workout at home?"

"Sure," his son replied without the least hesitation.

"Did you see those rollbacks?" Hugh asked Ethan. Ethan nodded.

"What are rollbacks?" Donny asked.

"Those spins and sharp turns Cochise made every time I switched direction. It means he was probably a cutting horse before your folks bought him."

"Oh. I thought he was just trying to scrape me off sometimes by throwing me off balance."

"You'll need to watch for that," Hugh said. "Tighten your legs when you make a turn. Otherwise you'll kiss the ground and end up being a dirt angel."

Donny laughed, the sound as brilliant as water. He had a hell of a smile when he wasn't trying so hard to be a grown-up. It would be so easy to love this kid, Ethan thought. The easiest thing he'd ever done.

A cell phone rang, and Donny snatched it out of his jeans pocket. He looked at the screen, then his watch. His eyes widened. "Oh, crap, it's Mom," he said in a whisper, as though Cassie could hear him. "I was supposed to be home twenty minutes ago. She's fixing meat loaf for dinner, and she hates when it gets dried out."

"I thought you'd gone vegetarian?" Ethan said.

"I decided to wait until after the Fourth of July. Dad makes the best barbecue sauce in Texas." He gave Ethan a hopeful look, offering the phone. "You want to help me out here? Make some excuse why I'm late?"

Ethan held up both hands as though surrendering. "Sorry. You're on your own. I never mess with moms and their meat loaf."

"Want me to ask her if you can come to dinner?"

Oh, she'd love that, Ethan thought. He shook his head. "I appreciate the invite, but I don't think that's a good idea."

The phone continued to ring. With a sigh, Donny pressed a button, then lifted the cell to his ear. "Hi, Mom. You looking for me?"

The boy listened, fidgeting a little. He offered the men a put-upon eye roll. "Just goofing around at Ethan's place," he told his mother. After a few moments, he added, "No, I'm not. Yeah, he said I could call him that." The listening part got longer, and Ethan wondered what demands Cassie was making. From the look on Donny's face, the kid had heard them before. "Okay," he finally said. "I'll leave right now. Sure. Hold on." Unexpectedly, he held the phone out to Ethan. "She wants to talk to you."

Puzzled, Ethan took it. Did she intend to give him a lecture about keeping Donny late? He supposed he'd never figure out the protocol for a situation like this, but he was beginning not to care.

"Hi, Cassie," he said, in a deliberately upbeat tone. Pointedly, he added, "What a surprise to hear from you."

"What's Donny doing over there?"

"Picking up a few tips with Cochise. Just hanging with the guys."

"What guys?"

"My partner and Dad."

"Your father's there?" she asked, both surprise and some uneasiness in her voice.

Annoyance stretched its limbs inside Ethan's chest. She obviously remembered the complaints he'd had about Hugh all those years ago, how unfit he'd considered him as a father. But though his opinion hadn't changed much, Ethan didn't like the idea that Cassie was sitting in her fancy living room at the ranch, trying to control the situation from afar. Probably stewing about the fact that her son was in unsuitable company.

Too bad. "Didn't I tell you?" he said. "Dad showed up here. He's helping out for the time being."

There was nothing but silence on the line. Ethan

could imagine her thoughts. Eventually she said in all seriousness, "We need to talk."

"Isn't that what we're doing?" he asked.

"Not right now. Later. Privately." He recognized the irritation that had slipped into her tone, and thought he could guess the expression on her face at that moment. "Send Donny home, then give me a call tonight. Eight o'clock."

Ethan felt he had matured in a lot of ways over the years. But unless they were coming from his boss, he still didn't appreciate taking orders without so much as a "please" or "thank you." Considering the circumstances, he didn't see why he shouldn't resent it now. "Dinner tonight?" he asked, taking perverse delight in having a little fun with her. "I think that's a wonderful idea. I'll pick you up at eight, then."

"What? I didn't say anything about having dinner—"

"You're right," he said, not giving her a chance to respond. "We do have so much to talk about. We barely scratched the surface the other night."

"Ethan, this is an absurd conversation. You can't force me to have dinner with you. Not tonight or any other night."

"All righty. I'll see you at eight." He shut the phone on her protest and handed it back to Donny. "Better ride, partner. Your meat loaf's getting cold."

The boy gave him an odd look as he climbed into the saddle. Before he could ask any questions, Ethan stepped back, waved goodbye and began looping the lunge lead in his hands. A moment later, Donny galloped away.

"Don't forget to cool him down!" he called out.

"Will do," Donny shouted back. "Thanks for all the help!"

Feeling pretty good, Ethan resumed gathering gear. He looked up to find Quintin smiling at him.

"Nice kid," his partner remarked.

"Yeah," Ethan replied, then realized he was smiling, too.

Hugh trooped off to clear away the trash from the campsite, tossing cups and chip bags into a receptacle that could be dumped in town when Ethan went back to the hotel.

Quintin came to stand shoulder to shoulder with Ethan in the late afternoon sunlight. "Dinner with the enemy?" he said, his tone conspiratorial. "Better watch out for poison in your food. They say that's a woman's weapon of choice."

"If I don't show up tomorrow morning, call the cops."

"If you don't show up tomorrow morning," Quintin countered with a sly grin, "I'll know where to find you both. With a Do Not Disturb sign on the knob, I'm guessing."

CHAPTER TEN

TEN MINUTES LATER Ethan was ready to leave. He'd grabbed a few things from the tent and settled them into the back of his truck. If he was really going to take Cassie to dinner at eight, he'd need a shower at his hotel and a change of clothes.

"You guys set for tonight?" he asked.

Quintin nodded, but Hugh spoke up. "Actually, I was wondering if you could give me a ride into town. I have some business I need to take care of."

The request was the first real favor Hugh had asked of him, and Ethan had to admit he came close to refusing. He didn't like spending time alone with his father. Every moment with the man seemed to stretch on forever. Besides, he was feeling good right now. *Light-headed* was the word that came to mind, and he didn't want that to change.

But what could he say without looking churlish? It was Saturday night, and a man needed a break once in a while. Of course, that was part of what worried him. His father had been an expert at getting into trouble, and drunken weekend brawls had always been his favorite pastime. AA or not, his dad had never been known for keeping promises.

But remembering the letter he'd found under the

mattress, Ethan just didn't have the heart or energy to say no.

The drive to Beaumont took only ten minutes, but sure enough, with his father beside him in the front seat, it seemed endless. Ethan stared ahead intently, as though the meager Saturday traffic was rush hour in Manhattan. Hugh did the same, though every so often Ethan could feel the older man's gaze, like a metal currycomb being dragged over every nerve ending in his body.

His dad's hands were stretched out in front of him, resting on his knees. He seemed preternaturally calm, sitting there like that. Ethan didn't like it. In the old days, Hugh had never had that kind of silent self-containment.

He wondered briefly if his father suspected he'd read that letter, but supposed it was his own guilty conscience making him think that. Just to stick his finger in his own eye, Ethan shifted his gaze from the road long enough to give Hugh a close look.

"You're pretty quiet," he remarked. "Something on your mind?"

"Not much. Something on yours?"

"Beaumont isn't like New Orleans. Not much action, if that's what you're looking for."

"I suppose if a person's determined, they can still get into trouble."

Inwardly, Ethan grimaced. He should have known he'd never get a straight answer out of his father. Better to finish the drive in complete silence.

"Who's this Cassie woman?" Hugh asked suddenly.

Oh, hell. No way was Ethan going to have *that* discussion. He shrugged. "An old friend. I used to work for her dad years ago."

Hugh turned to stare at Ethan. "Is she pretty?"

"She's had her share of admirers."

"Were you one of them?"

"I was the hired help," he replied carefully. He decided that a touch of truth would work best. "The boss's daughter is always off-limits to the mongrel hordes."

"I can't imagine that stopping you." His father absorbed the information for a few moments. Finally, he said, "I like her son. That Donny."

Ethan's stomach did a flip. The conversation was going downhill. He didn't really want to talk about Cassie, but he *definitely* didn't want to discuss Donny. He made a yes-no movement with his head, aiming for nonchalance. "He seems all right."

"He's smart," Hugh commented, his glance finding Ethan again, and this time his sharpened look seemed to have developed needlelike precision. "You know who he reminds me of?"

"No," Ethan replied, barely able to get the word out.

"You."

He feigned surprise, while his stomach went from flips right into a nosedive. "Really? I don't see it."

"He's got a good riding seat. Lots of control in his grip. Good posture, same as yours. When you were his age, you looked like a poster boy for riding lessons."

Ethan was breathing again. "I imagine he's been around horses all his life. I'll bet his dad had him on a pony before the kid could walk," he added, remembering that photograph of Josh and Donny in the Flying M's living room.

"Good for him, then," Hugh said. "You live in Texas,

you need to know how to ride. A father should see to things like that for his son."

Ethan darted a quick glance in Hugh's direction. If the man meant anything by that remark, he didn't show it.

To Ethan's relief, the rest of the trip into Beaumont was silent. Hugh asked to be let out near the entertainment complex on touristy Crockett Street, leaving Ethan to wonder what mischief his father had in mind. Nothing too bad, he hoped. He realized suddenly that, in spite of everything, he'd hate like hell to have to fire him tomorrow.

I need the help too badly, he told himself. *That's all.*

At the turnoff to Ethan's hotel, Hugh got out. He slapped his hand on the truck roof. "Thanks for the lift, son. I'll see you tomorrow."

Ethan nodded and watched him back away and disappear into the growing crowd heading out for a fun Saturday night.

If the man was set on getting into trouble, there was nothing Ethan could do about it, really. One way or another, Hugh would do what he wanted. He always had. Anytime Ethan had tried to help, he'd gotten the worst end of Hugh's temper for doing so.

He pulled away from the curb, determined not to give his father another thought. He had better things to think about this evening. Right now, there just wasn't enough room in his head to worry about Hugh, when anticipation of dinner with Cassie had moved in and staked a claim on nearly every crack and crevice in his thoughts.

Tomorrow was soon enough to deal with his dad. Tonight, if at all possible, he intended to turn back time.

CASSIE WORE BLACK, telling herself it matched her mood. She chose a high neck and long sleeves in spite of the heat of the day, which would keep the evening humid and unpleasant. The severe lines made her look taller, more dignified and definitely in command.

Without thinking, she lifted a bottle of her favorite perfume from her dressing table and dabbed a touch behind her ear. Then, just as quickly, she snatched up a tissue and wiped it away, annoyed with her inability to see this night for what it really was.

She jerked the zipper up the back of her dress. *This is not a date. Dinner. A meeting to discuss Donny. Nothing more. I am in control here.*

Too bad her nervous system didn't seem to be getting the message. How could both dread and excitement be pooled in the pit of her stomach? She could feel her pulse throbbing in her throat already, and Ethan hadn't even picked her up yet!

She should pull on some sweats, refuse to go. He couldn't force her to have dinner with him.

But even as she had the thought, she rejected it. She refused to have him think her a coward. Besides, they really did have to discuss the meeting she had had with Josh. Considering that they needed Ethan's cooperation with their plan, she ought to be trying to Mata Hari him. There were obviously still sparks between them. She should take advantage of that.

Unfortunately, if she succeeded in turning him into a salivating slave, there was a very real possibility she'd end up in an equally bad state. She didn't have to try very hard to recall the way she'd always reacted to Ethan's caresses. They could wind through her veins like a ribbon of silk, leaving her gasping. How could she convince him to do what she wanted when she couldn't even draw a breath?

Besides, she couldn't imagine Ethan becoming any woman's salivating slave. *Bad idea, Cassandra. Stick with the plan.*

And if that didn't work? Did Josh still have that wood chipper?

"Mom?"

The door to her bedroom stood ajar, and Donny stuck his head around it. His eyes widened a little when he saw her. There weren't many occasions around the ranch for her to get dressed up.

"Ethan's here," he said.

"Thanks. Will you tell him I'll be right down?"

He nodded, but continued to stand at the door. "You look nice. Is Dad meeting up with you?"

"No."

"How come you didn't just invite Ethan over to have meat loaf?"

Because he's a lying skunk who tricked me into this, she wanted to say. Instead, she just smiled. "It's nice to get out of the house once in a while. And we'd have bored you to death with all our stories about the old days."

She put on earrings, small golden studs that Donny had given her for her last birthday. She'd use them for luck, and a reminder of the true purpose of tonight's dinner.

"So, uh, is this a date?" Donny asked.

Cassie swung around. "No," she said, more sharply than she intended. "Absolutely not. Why do you ask?"

He shrugged. "Well…you do look pretty bitchin'."

"Donny! I don't like that word."

"Sorry! Doesn't mean it isn't true, though."

Momentarily, Cassie closed her eyes, trying to find the quiet center in her head where she went to draw strength. No luck. Finally, she crossed the room and took Donny by the shoulders.

"This is not a date," she told him again. "This is just a nice evening with an old friend. Understand?"

He looked so vulnerable suddenly, so young, but he nodded quickly and set his jaw. "It's all right, you know. It's not like I don't expect men to ever hit on you again now that…you're not with Dad. I don't want you to end up like some old ghost in a horror movie, floating around the ranch looking for someone to care about you."

Cassie's throat tightened with love. She shook her head at him, offering a smile. "I suppose I should find that worry very thoughtful. But I promise, I won't become a ghost."

He looked annoyed. "I can't say it right, but you know what I mean. I guess I'm just wondering when things will really start to change." He grimaced. "In a way, I sorta wish they would, just so we could get over it."

Lovingly, she ran her hand down the side of his face. For once he didn't pull away, embarrassed. This sweet, sweet boy. How would she ever survive the loss of him, even for a weekend? "Our lives are changing every day, honey. You're growing up, turning into the most terrifically charming, intelligent, handsome son I could ever have hoped for. But there's one thing that will never change, and that's my love for you."

Donny's answering smile was endearingly off center and just a bit shaky. He flushed, and she pulled away before he could feel any more awkward.

"Now go tell our guest that I'll be right down."

"Later can I watch TV?"

"No. You still have exams this week, and don't think I've forgotten about that call from your school. I've talked it over with your father and we haven't decided on a punishment yet."

Yesterday the principal had phoned to say that Donny had gotten into a fight with another boy. It was about something stupid and the whole situation was nothing she would have expected from her son.

Donny looked sullen. "They're making a big deal out of nothing. Neither one of us even got a black eye."

"But you started it. You're lucky you didn't get expelled."

"Can I at least spend some time down at the barn?"

"No."

"Is that why Mecerdes is staying late?" Donny asked, his tone full of resentment. "To be my jailer?"

"Yes, exactly," Cassie replied with a Mom look. "Tomorrow we're putting up bars in your room."

He made a face and escaped, thundering down the stairs just as he had when he'd been eight, racing toward Christmas presents.

Cassie picked up her clutch purse and took one last look in the mirror. She swept a stray lock of hair back into the twist she'd managed earlier. *Strong,* she reminded herself firmly. She had no idea how tonight would go, exactly, but she could handle this. She'd be pleasant. But strong.

"Come on, Cassandra," she muttered to her image. "It's time to show that wretched man he's not dealing with some future ghost."

FOR DONNY'S SAKE, they kept the conversation in the oak-lined foyer impersonal and polite. Just two old friends going out to dinner. She kissed Donny good-night and gave one last, meaningful look to Mercedes. The housekeeper nodded slightly.

It wasn't until Ethan had helped her into the passenger side of his truck that Cassie's heart began to speed up. It raced harder as she watched him walk around the front of the vehicle to get in the other side.

He looked good enough to frame. Clean-shaven, with hair as sinfully dark as rich mahogany. There were perfect creases in his trousers, but you'd hardly notice them for the way his white cotton shirt stretched across that broad chest.

When he settled into the driver's seat, he didn't start the engine. Instead, he turned to give her a blatant, thorough once-over, from the tips of her shoes to the top of her French twist.

He smiled. "You look very…elegant."

She could tell right away this night would be difficult. She didn't like the way he said that—as though he knew perfectly well that her defense shields had been raised, and he thought she was wasting her time.

She lifted her chin. "According to Donny, the word is *bitchin'*. Did you teach him that?"

"No."

She swung her gaze in his direction long enough to give him a skeptical look.

He held up a few fingers. "Scout's honor."

"I seriously doubt you were ever a Scout. If anything, you were the…the anti-Scout."

He laughed. "Maybe so, but I'm willing to bet he picked that word up from his friends. And probably a few things worse." In a voice threaded with amusement Ethan added, "But he's right."

"Thank you." She glanced out the side window. So much for the funereal black being a turnoff.

"I'm a little surprised," Ethan remarked, drawing her attention back to him. "I thought you'd engineer a way to include Josh this evening."

"Josh is in Houston tonight. A cattlemen's meeting."

"No Sir Lancelot, huh? You'll have to manage without his protection."

"I don't need him to protect me from you," she announced, a hint of defiance in her voice. Her eyes met his with a stab of impatience. "Are we going to sit here all night, or are we going to eat? I'm getting hungry."

Still smiling, he shook his head and started the engine. In a short time they reached the bottom of the front drive. Overhead, the Flying M's iron logo stood out starkly against a blue velvet sky.

"Steak all right with you?" Ethan asked, letting the truck idle.

"Fine."

"I thought we'd head back to my hotel. They have a pretty nice restaurant that serves a mean filet."

Of course. Ethan never had been one to waste time. "Your hotel?" she asked, keeping her expression cool and her tone a mocking drawl. "That's pretty obvious, isn't it? Even for you."

Lines spread from the corners of his eyes like tiny peacock tails. "You're a very suspicious woman."

"Around you, it pays to be."

He threw the gearshift into Park, then turned slightly toward her. "Look," he said, drawing a deep breath. He sat still a moment, as though waiting for the additional oxygen to calm him. "I'm not going into this evening with any hidden agenda. I want to share a bottle of wine with you. I want us to enjoy a meal together. I want good company after a hard day's work. In spite of our latest difficulties, I remember that that used to be you." Finally, he smiled again, that tilt of his mouth that always made her skin feel hot. "If something develops before the night is over, so be it. I'd be delighted."

His words had an eroding effect on her resolve, but she mustn't, *must not,* allow it. "Disappointed is more like what you'll be. Nothing's going to *develop.*"

"Don't be so sure. The sizzle's still there between us, and you know it."

"It is not."

"Try to confine your denials to something I can believe."

She looked away, but he startled her by reaching across the distance to catch her chin. He leaned closer, near enough that she breathed in the scent of woods and wind and citrus in his aftershave. Even by the pale light of the truck dashboard she could see the desire in his eyes. There was nothing between them but the night and a sudden, sweet hunger.

"Can't we just let everything go for a little while?" His voice rolled over her like a warm shower. "You want this as much as I do." It was not a question.

Somehow she found a shred of willpower. Enough to keep her voice firm, at least. "Maybe, but I'm not crazy enough to act on every impulse."

"How can we not? We're about to fulfill our fantasies."

"What fantasy would that be? The one where you kidnap a woman against her will?"

His fingers left her chin. He settled back in his seat. She couldn't tell if he was angry, amused or merely feeling thwarted. "Surely you remember how often we used to talk about having dinner away from the ranch like two normal people? An actual date. But there was no way that could happen with your dad around."

"He meant well. He just wanted to protect me from…"

Ethan lifted one brow. "From lowlifes like me?"

His words sank through Cassie like lead in quicksand. Years ago she'd had a talk with Josh about the night of the accident. He'd told her what her father had said to Ethan in the emergency room, how vicious he'd been. She could only chalk it up to worry over her, but it was still embarrassing.

Ethan remained silent, waiting.

"All right," she said helplessly. "You win. Let's have a nice evening of wine and food and conversation. Before the night's over, we'll talk about Donny. After that…" She shrugged, as though the outcome made no difference to her one way or the other.

She crossed her arms over her breasts, as though hugging herself. Or holding herself together, she thought grimly. Really, it was ridiculous. They weren't even off Flying M property yet, and she was making concessions.

Laughter tugged at Ethan's lips, but he nodded slowly and pulled out of the drive, heading for downtown Beaumont.

CHAPTER ELEVEN

THE HOTEL'S RESTAURANT was as Ethan had said, dim and classy and smelling deliciously of sauces. The maître d' seemed to know him, flashing a professional smile and leading them to a table near the windows that overlooked a pretty atrium.

After a waiter had left them with oversize menus, the sommelier came to the table. Cassie unfolded the cloth napkin and carefully spread it over her lap while Ethan ordered a bottle of burgundy she'd never heard of.

They placed their orders—the house specialty. The wine came. After it had been uncorked, tasted by Ethan, and a glass poured for each of them, Cassie took a sip. She didn't know much about wine, but it slipped over her tongue like warm satin. She set the goblet down and smiled at him. "I didn't realize you'd become a wine connoisseur."

"Hardly," he answered with a self-deprecating snort. "I suppose I can find my way around a wine list now. I once worked on the security detail for a Saudi prince in Dubai who was determined to educate us about wine."

"Dubai. Did you like it there?"

"Not particularly. Too dry and dusty. I enjoyed Europe. All that history around every corner. And New Zealand. Very lush. Some amazing scenery."

Cassie wondered how many different places he'd

been over the years. Dozens? A lot, no doubt. What a life he must have had. "We used to talk so often about traveling," she said. "You've probably been everywhere, haven't you?"

"Enough. Most of the jobs I took were overseas, but I can't say I ever fell in love with any place so much that I wanted to live there forever."

"Still, I envy that."

They spent some time talking about various cities he'd lived in, stories about people and experiences that Cassie found fascinating, all the more so because Ethan knew how to weave a tale. She remembered that about him—that ability to bring her dreams to life with just a few well-chosen words.

When the conversation wound down, he tilted his head at her. "What about you? You ever leave the Flying M?"

"Oh, we've been on family vacations. The Grand Canyon. Disney World. When your life is centered around children, it's a little different." She tipped her wineglass and stared into the ruby-colored liquid. "Josh is very organized. He never leaves anything to chance. That can sometimes make traveling a bit... unexciting."

She frowned. That had sounded like a complaint. Not fair to Josh, really, because he'd always been the one to plan their holidays down to the smallest detail, just so she could have it easy. He was such a good man, filled with humor, kindness, deep intelligence. Why couldn't she have loved him the way he'd deserved?

Their steaks arrived, still sizzling from the grill and cooked perfectly. As Cassie cut into her meat, Ethan poured them both another glass of wine. She didn't object. If he thought he could get her drunk enough to lose all inhibitions, he'd be sadly disappointed, just as she'd promised.

She lifted her glass. "Cheers," she said, and downed a good swallow. The wine hit her stomach, setting off another warm glow.

He gave her a look of wry amusement. "You should probably go easy on that. The last thing I want to do tonight is have to carry you back to my room."

"I thought that's *exactly* where you wanted me to end up. Your room."

"Not passed out cold."

She slipped a bit of steak onto her fork. "Don't worry. I've never been drunk in my life. I have my father's iron stomach."

"I didn't know that about you."

She waved her knife with a flourish. "There are hundreds of things you don't know about me."

"I don't think we ever had enough time to find out," he said, tossing her a thoughtful look. More seriously, he added, "I wish it had been different."

She gazed down at the napkin on her lap. For a moment she wondered if she'd imagined the sadness she'd heard in his voice. How deep were his regrets about their shared past? For her, it seemed to have taken ages to heal, and she'd had Donny to soften the blow of lost love. But what had Ethan had?

Suddenly too curious to keep from asking, she lifted her head. "Have you ever been married?"

"No."

"Why not?"

His mouth moved as though he found the topic unpleasant. "Pretty simple, really. I never met anyone I could envision coming home to every night."

"Not even close?"

"Once, years ago. But it didn't last."

"What went wrong?"

His gaze captured hers with laserlike focus. "She wasn't you," he replied simply.

Cassie flinched before she could stop herself. If he was lying, he made a convincing show. In the blue depths of his eyes, there was a shining, unequivocal truth. She recognized it, but she wasn't sure how to negotiate it.

She turned her head away. "Please don't say things like that."

"Why?"

"Because it makes me uncomfortable."

"Why should it? You think just because I ditched this town thirteen years ago I stopped loving you that night? It took me a long time to accept that we weren't going to be together for the rest of our lives."

She looked back at him and leaned forward slightly. "We were very young, Ethan."

"So love has some sort of expiration date?"

"I think people grow up and move on. They make new lives for themselves. Ones that have meaning and purpose."

"You mean like raising a child."

"That's one way."

He made a derogatory chuffing sound. "I'd be more inclined to take comfort in that fact if I'd ever been allowed to be part of Donny's life."

She skated her wineglass around in a small circle on the tablecloth, buying time while she searched for something to say. Nothing brilliant came to her. "I'm sorry," she said at last. "I never meant to hurt you. It was just…a solution. And at the time, I was desperate for one."

He shook his head, as though weary of this conversation. "What's done is done. But I want to make it right now, Cass. And I'm tired of waiting for you and Josh to come to the table with a proposal."

She sat up straighter, glad to get back to business and discuss the things that needed to be resolved between them. "I know. That's why I called you today. I wanted to talk about some decisions Josh and I have made."

Ethan set his fork down, dabbed his lips with his napkin, then gave her his full attention. "I'm listening."

"First off, I want to let you know that Josh and Donny are going camping this weekend. A little one-on-one guy-time together. They've been planning it for ages, and I don't think they should cancel it."

"How is that supposed to help me?"

"Josh plans to talk to Donny, explain things better. Like why our divorce doesn't mean we love him any less."

"Is he going to tell Donny that I'm his father?"

"No."

Ethan frowned. "Sounds peachy. A little father-son bonding. I don't see how that's going to get us to a solution."

"Whether it does or not," she said firmly, "I think we owe Josh that time. He's been there for Donny every step of the way. He shouldn't be pushed out of the picture just because you've come back. I'm not going to allow it."

Seconds ticked away as Ethan stared at his wine-glass as though it held the secrets of the universe. His annoyance was apparent in the stern focus on his face and the way his jaw twitched. She could guess his thoughts. He probably envied and resented the connection between Josh and Donny and the fact that there was absolutely nothing he could do about it.

Finally, he nodded slowly. "Agreed," he said. "What's part two of the plan?"

One obstacle down. One to go. The big one. She felt the painful sweep of her blood in her veins. It seemed likely she'd get a cold reception from Ethan over her and Josh's next decision. For courage, she took another sip of wine, then gave him her steadiest look.

"Josh and I are going to take Donny to see a child psychologist."

Ethan jerked upright. She felt his shock coming toward her like humidity on a summer day. "You think he needs a shrink?"

"I think we should take advantage of whatever expertise is out there to help us. Donny is at a very critical age, Ethan. We can't afford to mess this up."

"Every day there are thousands of kids in this country who are faced with parents getting a divorce. Fathers walk out on the family. Mothers abuse them. They don't get help from a psychiatrist, and they still turn out just fine."

"This isn't just about handling the divorce. I want a professional there when we tell him you're his father."

"You think Donny's going to be that undone to find out he's related to me?"

She heard the hurt in that question, and the anger. "I think it will come as a shock to him, no matter who I said was his father."

Ethan seemed to be thinking that over. She said

nothing, just continued to look at him with steel in her posture. If the evening was going to go off the rails, this would be the time. But she and Josh had talked this over thoroughly, and they were adamant that professional help could get Donny through this.

The waiter came to refill water glasses and take away plates. "Would you like to see the dessert menu?"

"Give us a minute, please." Ethan waved him away, then shook his head with a flicker of impatience. "Why this sudden desire for outside help?"

"I told you that he skipped school and then lied to us about it. Yesterday he got into a fight with a kid in one of his classes. Nothing more than a tussle, from the sound of it, but he definitely started it."

"So? Boys fight."

"My son doesn't pick on other children. This kind of behavior is so unlike him, and it scares me. Even Josh was surprised."

"You're being overly cautious. Donny can handle the idea of me being his father. Is this Josh's idea? Some kind of stall tactic?"

"I've told you we won't do that. But I'd like to point out that you've been with Donny very seldom, so you're hardly the best judge of what he needs."

"Cass, I grew up with parents who were role models for dysfunctional families. All things considered, I think I turned out all right."

"Let me ask you something," she said, leaning forward for emphasis and to keep anyone from overhearing. "When your father was abusing both you and your mother, when everything was going to hell for you at home, wouldn't you have been glad to have someone to talk to about it? Some impartial third party you felt you could trust, who'd just listen and help you figure things out?"

She caught the reflection of his thoughts in his face. Considering, but still not convinced. "This is not the same situation," he said.

"Maybe not. But we could benefit from that same level of expertise. Please, Ethan. I want to do this right."

"So take him to a session if it will make you both feel better," he said at last, with a pinch of resentment in his voice.

She grimaced. "I'm afraid it will be a little more complicated than that."

"In what way?"

She slipped a business card out of her purse and slid it across the table. "I've done some research. Dr. Parker comes highly recommended, and he's the one I'd like to have work with Donny after we tell him."

"So?"

"So, the soonest I can get an appointment is in three weeks."

He pushed back his hair with a wide, reckless gesture. "Hell, no. I'm not sitting for three weeks in the background like a beggar, waiting for whatever scraps you and Josh decide to throw my way. Find someone else."

"I don't want anyone else," she replied, trying to keep warmth and sympathy in her tone so as not to ruin the small concessions he'd already made. "I want what's best for Donny. And if you really care about him, that's what you'll want, too. I'm not suggesting you sit on the sidelines. In fact, I think you'll need to play a significant role in all this." She wet her lips, suddenly feeling a desperate need to be done with the conversation. "I think it would help if you go with us to meet Dr. Parker. He can tell us the best way to handle this."

Ethan looked incredulous and swore softly under his breath. "I hate that psychobabble crap."

She gave him a soft, understanding smile. "I knew you'd say something like that. That's why I wanted to tell you in person."

"Mr. Rafferty."

Having been completely absorbed in their discussion, they both looked up, surprised to find that one of the hotel employees had arrived at the table. He made a half bow, and Cassie saw from his name badge that he was the front desk manager.

"What can I do for you, Chuck?"

"I'm sorry to disturb you, but I wonder if you could come with me. It's about an older gentleman. He claims to be your father."

Cassie saw Ethan stiffen. "What about him?"

"It seems he's run into a bit of trouble. I'm afraid it's going to get ugly if something isn't done. Since you're a valued guest here, I thought you should know. Before we have to summon the police."

Ethan stood immediately, tossing his napkin into his chair. "Where is he?"

"The hotel bar, sir."

Turning back to Cassie, Ethan gave her a short smile. "Order dessert. I'll be back as soon as I can."

She watched him stride away with Chuck. She remained where she was, speculating on what drama his father had managed to get himself involved in. Nothing good, she was sure. Ethan hadn't talked about his family much, but she'd been a good listener, and there had been no mistaking the hurt in his features every time Hugh

Rafferty's name had come up. Today, when he'd told her that his father was working for him, she'd been really surprised.

Sighing heavily, she let her heart settle. Now that they were no longer in the middle of a heated discussion, she could regroup. If Ethan still wanted to disagree with her about a psychologist for Donny when he returned, she'd be ready for round two, if necessary.

The waiter reappeared. "Dessert now, miss?"

She glanced toward the front entrance of the restaurant. The bar was right next door, but there was no sign of Ethan. Had he run into real trouble with his father? Was there something she could do to help? She had to admit she was curious as hell about the man who was Donny's grandfather. Was he as bad as she feared?

In the distance she heard raised voices, then the sound of glass breaking.

A second later, Cassie was on her feet.

CHAPTER TWELVE

THE HOTEL BAR WAS a typical cowboy hangout, with saddles and lassos and longhorn heads mounted on the walls. It took a moment for Cassie's eyes to adjust to the meager light, but it wasn't hard to find Ethan and his father. The bar wasn't crowded, but every head in the place was turned toward the raised voices coming from one brightly lit corner in the rear of the room.

A poker table sat within a few feet of the bar. Chips and money lay scattered across the green felt, but no one was seated.

Ethan had one hand around the arm of a shorter, older man, whom Cassie assumed was his father. Chuck, the front desk manager, was directing a bartender to clear up broken glass from beer bottles that lay shattered on the floor. Two other men stood a few feet from them. They were dressed casually, like golfers just off the course. Their faces were flushed with anger, their stances like gladiators preparing to meet the tigers head-on.

Cassie recognized them immediately. Randy and Blake Delmar, two of Beaumont's more prominent citizens since their father had died and left them a small fortune. The brothers had gone to school with Cassie, and were two of the most annoying jerks she'd ever known.

Ethan's father gestured wildly toward the brothers.

"Don't tell me I'm a crazy old fool! I was playing poker before you were born, you little snot."

"Dad!" Ethan said sharply. "Stop."

"I've listened to about all of this I intend to," Randy replied, leaning to scoop money from the table.

He reared back as Hugh Rafferty struggled to escape his son's restraining hand. "You touch that pot—either one of you—and I'll be all over you like a cheap suit."

Blake, only slightly less aggressive than his brother, swore softly. "This is ridiculous." He turned toward Chuck. "Call the police."

"Yeah, call 'em," Hugh encouraged. "We'll see what they say when I tell them that you and your brother here have been card-swapping all night." He looked at Ethan. "Some upstanding citizens they got in this town."

"Sit down," Ethan ordered in a harsh command, and Hugh plopped into one of the chairs. From where Cassie stood, she could tell that both father and son were vibrating with tension. Ethan swung back to the Delmar brothers. "My father has a tendency—"

"Don't you dare apologize for me!" Hugh shouted, popping back up like a jack-in-the-box to grab Ethan's attention. "These two have been colluding since we started. You think I don't recognize some of the same tricks I used to use to win a pot? Their shoulders have been bobbing all night, as they swapped cards under the table. I tried to let it go—everybody cheats once in a while—but now they've started false flushing." He sneered at the brothers. "You think I'm too feeble to spot a diamond stuck in the middle of hearts? Got to flash it faster than that, my boy."

"You don't know what you're talking about," Randy said, but Cassie noticed that his face went considerably redder. It wouldn't surprise her if the Delmars had been cheating. They might be rich, but honorable they were not.

Hugh seemed more interested in convincing Ethan than fighting with the brothers. He shook his head in abstract denial. "I'm telling the truth, son," he said. "It wasn't that hard to spot—these two asses haven't got the IQ of a watermelon between them."

Randy's fists balled, and he made a move in Hugh's direction. "Listen here, you old bastard—"

Ethan swung around. His blue eyes had gone to flint. "Wait a minute—"

There was no time to think it over. Taking a deep breath, Cassie stepped into the tight circle of angry men. "Hello, Randy. Blake."

Everyone turned to look at her. In surprise mostly, though there was a short, nervous laugh from Randy and a raised eyebrow from Hugh Rafferty. She refused to glance Ethan's way, certain she'd see disapproval.

"Cassandra," Blake Delmar said. "What are you doing here?"

"I'm just an impartial observer who'd like to suggest a little common sense." She focused on the brothers. "You fellows don't really want the police called, do you? Reports to fill out, all those annoying questions. Think of the adverse publicity." She turned to Blake. "Aren't you thinking of running for town councilman in November?"

Blake thought that over a mere second or two, then touched his brother's arm. "Let it go, Randy. Give him the pot and let's get out of here."

"I don't like being called a cheat," Randy replied.

Wouldn't be the first time, Cassie thought. In high

school, Randy had been quite famous for his innovative ways of cheating on exams. "Of course not. But, Randy, let's be realistic." She pointed back to Hugh. "This man thinks you and Blake were dishonest, and he doesn't strike me as the kind of person who'll just walk away from that."

"You're right." Hugh spoke up in a voice that carried across the room to more than a dozen interested ears. "I certainly will not."

"So," Cassie said in a lower voice, "wouldn't it be better to call an end to this? You know people will talk, and all that old foolishness about you in high school will start circulating again, just when you thought it was forgotten."

Randy stared at her. He chewed the inside of his mouth, thinking. In a few moments, he tossed the chips on the poker table. He gave Hugh his most insulting smile. "Fine. Keep it, old man. You obviously need it more than I do." He pushed Blake ahead of him. "Let's go."

The brothers left the bar and a relieved-looking Chuck returned to the front desk. Customers, probably disappointed that the fight had ended without blows, went back to sipping their drinks.

Hugh Rafferty gathered the money from the center of the table. It wasn't a huge pot, but probably worth his determination not to lose it. From the looks of him, he wasn't a man of considerable means.

When he straightened, he offered her a smile that ran ear to ear. "Thank you, young lady. I appreciate the help."

"You're welcome. Were they really cheating?"

"Crooked as corkscrews, the both of them," he said

with a knowing wink. He held out his hand. "I'm Hugh Rafferty. You must be Donny's mom."

"Cassie Wheeler. Nice to meet you," she replied. She had yet to glance at Ethan. In a way, she was afraid to. "I've heard a lot about you."

"Nothing good, I'll wager."

Beside them, Ethan spoke up as he held out his hotel room key to his father. "Why don't you go upstairs? You can have the second bed tonight instead of going back to camp."

"Why, thank you," Hugh replied with a blink of surprise. He took the key and then turned to Cassie again. "I've slept on a floor often enough and been glad to have it, but I have to admit a nice, soft bed would feel mighty good."

They watched him head out of the bar while they followed more slowly. By the time they reached the lobby, Hugh Rafferty was just getting on the elevator. He waved at them, smiling broadly, as though he didn't have a care in the world.

Cassie glanced up at Ethan. His features were tight, and he seemed to radiate tension. "So that's the infamous Hugh Rafferty, huh?"

"What the hell were you doing?" he asked with gritted teeth. "I told you to wait for me in the restaurant."

She felt a swift upward surge of irritation. "Well, I decided not to. And I *think* I effectively diffused the situation, so maybe you ought to be thanking me instead of berating me."

"Thank you, but don't you realize that you could have been hurt if fists started flying?"

"They didn't," she argued back. She made a face at him. "Stop acting like a macho movie hero." She sighed, feeling surprisingly invigorated. "That's the most excitement I've had in years. But your father really shouldn't play cards with people like the Delmar brothers."

"Why? Because he's socially beneath them?"

"What?" She looked at him in sudden confusion. "No. Because the Delmars might have money, but they're too stupid to cheat someone for long. Especially someone who clearly knows more about poker than they do."

Ethan said nothing to that. They reached a short corridor that led back to the restaurant. The silence seemed filled with choking, forbidden things.

"Your father—he's different than I expected."

"He claims he's a reformed man, although that doesn't seem to apply to gambling," Ethan muttered sourly. Then, as though he regretted those words, he turned her to face him, suddenly all smiles. "Shall we go back to the dining room and have dessert?"

She grimaced. "Actually, I think maybe we should call it a night."

He moved so quickly. One moment they were in the corridor, the next, he'd pulled her into a leafy alcove meant to offer just this kind of privacy.

His arms went around her. She didn't pull away. He gave her a long, assessing look that made her blush. "I don't want tonight to end this way," he said softly.

"Tough luck, cowboy. Looks like we're not sharing a bed tonight. Not with your father two feet away."

He frowned, seeing her point.

"Besides," she continued, "we were talking business. Will you agree to let Dr. Parker help us?"

"Cassie—"

"It's simple—yes or no?"

Ethan touched the back of his hand to her cheek. "If I say yes, will you give me a kiss?"

"That's blackmail," she managed to say, although her breathing had started to stumble.

"It's simple," he countered, parroting her own words back to her. "Yes or no?"

"No. But if you agree, I'll let *you* kiss *me*."

"Deal."

Slipping in beneath her defenses, he kissed her then. His need was a tangible thing, urgent and poignant. Her lips trembled in anticipation instead of outrage. It welcomed instead of repelled, and as their mouths collided in an explosion of heat and longing, she gloried in the assault of his tongue.

She wrapped her arms around his neck. Her hands were as shameless as his, desperate to coax him even closer. She felt his strong, hard body respond to the urgency she couldn't conceal. She let him lead the way, following without qualms or reservations. All the years of separation were gone in a flash. The old dreams she'd had as a girl still survived, tenaciously battling eviction. Desire, so long buried, overwhelmed her, settling into her fingers and toes.

They had temporarily ceased to care what overtook them, but soon enough they heard voices coming down the corridor. With a groan, Ethan released her, though they remained pressed against the shaded wall like desperadoes eager to escape watchful eyes.

When the voices faded, Ethan looked down at her. She knew that her face must be lit with amazement and ungovernable delight. "Wow," she said with a short laugh. "You take that sealed-with-a-kiss stuff seriously, don't you?"

"A bargain is a bargain." He tilted his head at her. "You know, I'll bet the hotel has other rooms just sitting empty."

Slowly, the fierce fire in her receded. She brought her hands up between them, feeling his heartbeat like a wild drum beneath her fingers. "Don't push it, Rafferty. I'm already way out of my comfort zone with you. I want to go home now."

He looked disappointed, but gave a small nod. "I'll have them bring my car around."

"That's not necessary. There's a cab stand outside. I'll take one home."

"That's silly. I'll drive you."

"Driving me home isn't what worries me," she told him as she slipped back into the corridor. "It's all the other things I know you're capable of." She headed toward the lobby, leaving him standing in the shady alcove.

AFTER SETTLING THE restaurant bill, Ethan went upstairs.

While he wasn't completely satisfied with the way the night had ended, he couldn't say he'd been entirely disappointed, either. He had wanted to end up with Cassie in his room, just the two of them, enjoying some alone time. But with that kiss in the corridor, she had responded just the way he had hoped she would.

Now, he wanted to see more than that short flash of passion. He wanted to see if the woman who seemed to live behind a locked door these days was still the girl he remembered.

Except for the bathroom light, the room lay in deep shadows. His father had taken the bed nearest the window. He lay on his side, turned away, no more than a long lump. Ethan hoped he was asleep. He had no desire to talk to him tonight. The dustup downstairs had reminded him too much of the old days.

Luck seemed to have deserted him. Almost as he had that thought, a voice came out of the darkness. "Sorry if I messed up your plans."

"Don't worry about it."

Ethan tossed his key on the dresser, sat on the edge of his bed and slipped off his shoes.

"Mrs. Wheeler seems like quite a catch."

"Uh-huh," Ethan replied, unwilling to carry on this conversation.

The bedsprings groaned as Hugh turned over. In another moment, the lamp switched on. Ethan looked back to see his dad levered up on one elbow. With mussed hair and a day's growth of beard, he looked older than he usually did.

Hugh gave him a shrewd glance. "Does the kid know you're his father?"

Ethan tried to keep his surprise from showing. No point in deceit. For all his faults, his father could read people like a book. "No," he said. "Not yet."

"You plan on telling him anytime soon?"

"We're working that out. Go to sleep. We have a busy day ahead of us tomorrow."

"Ah, so the topic's off-limits, I see. Well, it's your business, and I suppose you know best how to handle it."

Ethan didn't respond. He continued to undress. About the time he was ready to turn out the light, his father spoke up again. "Mind if I ask you another question?"

"I don't seem to be able to stop you."

Hugh swung his feet to the floor and wearily combed his fingers through his salt-and-pepper hair. His shoulders drooped. "Are you planning to give me the boot?"

Ethan couldn't have been more startled if he'd just found out they were sleeping on the moon. Frankly, the idea hadn't occurred to him. Pretty strange, really, considering that he'd been looking for days for a chance to send Hugh packing. Certainly, what had happened tonight should have provided that excuse.

"What makes you think I'd want to fire you?"

"Come on," Hugh replied. "Don't tell me you weren't seeing red down in the bar. I'm sorry you got called into my fight. I wouldn't have involved you. It was hotel management that wimped out."

"Why should there ever have to *be* a fight?" Ethan gave him an incredulous look. "You wouldn't have minded at all if those two Neanderthals had decided to duke it out with you, would you?"

"Yeah, I'd have minded. But I still know a few moves that would have had them flat on their backs."

Ethan shook his head. "I know you're working on the drinking, and—"

"I hope you noticed that I was drinking soda down there." When Ethan said nothing to that, he added a little desperately, "And the gambling… I don't do near as much as I used to. A friendly game once in a while. No cheating and no risking my whole paycheck. Can't afford it. My boss is kind of a cheapskate." He winked to take the sting out of the words.

"All right. I get it. You're a work in progress."

"Working on it every day. It's not easy, I can tell you."

Ethan gave him a serious look, a soft accusation. "You've got a lot to be forgiven for, Dad."

"I know."

They sat in dead silence for a long, long moment while memories fell around Ethan like an avalanche. This was someone who would have once pulled rings off a dead man's hands. He'd been abusive, made his wife so miserable that when she'd died from cancer she'd probably thanked God for taking her. Ethan had more anger inside him toward his father than he thought possible. And yet he couldn't help wanting to believe...

Anything was possible, wasn't it? Look how much his own life had changed just since he'd come here.

Ethan sat on the side of the bed, elbows on his knees, his head hanging down, trying to think. Finally, he glanced up at Hugh. "I want to ask you something, and I want you to tell me the truth."

"I have very few secrets these days."

"I'm serious."

"Go on."

"Why? Why are you a changed man? What brought on this epiphany after all those years of being one of the biggest bastards on the planet?"

His father didn't flinch at that description. He merely nodded sadly. "You're right to ask. It surprised the heck out of me, too. But it didn't happen like you think. It wasn't all of a sudden I woke up and knew I wanted to change. It took a few years."

"How?"

"I met a woman named Sondra." Hugh sat up farther, so that his back was against the headboard. "My drinking put me in the hospital a couple of years ago. She was a social worker there and she came to see me."

"You've had social workers try to help you before," Ethan said skeptically. "I remember them coming to the house. For all the good it did anyone."

"Sondra was different. She didn't preach or threaten or try to wring promises out of me. Her theory was that sometimes you just have to start over. 'Hugh,' she used to say, 'every day drops into your hands like a lump of clay waiting to be shaped into whatever you want.' After I got out of the hospital, I played along for a while, mostly 'cause I wanted to see more of her. She was about forty-five, pretty and, in spite of everything, she seemed to think I had potential."

A wave of what felt like resentment hit Ethan. His mother had been an attractive, caring woman, too, at one time. Before his father had leached all the love out of her. "I see," he said, because Hugh seemed to be waiting for him to speak.

The older man laughed a little. "No, I don't think you do. It wasn't just me chasing a skirt. Yeah, she was nice-looking, but not beautiful. It was her soul that could take your breath away. Like an earthbound angel."

"So you fell in love."

"We never called it that. Never slept together. And while I would have loved her forever, I'm not sure she felt the same way. She just had such a good heart, the best attitude and a way of making you feel like there were valid reasons to get up in the morning. It made me want to be around her all the time."

So it could all be chalked up to the love of a good woman? Ethan found that hard to swallow. Some of his cynicism must have been apparent on his face, because Hugh shook his head.

"I know what you're thinking," he said. "If I could

feel that way about a woman, why couldn't I have felt that way about your mom. But the truth is, son, your mother and me, we weren't ever gonna last long-term. We had plenty of passion in the beginning, but eventually, it wasn't enough. Your mom should have left me long before she got sick."

"Or maybe you should have stopped making us all so miserable." Ethan couldn't help it; there was the suggestion of knives in every word. Hugh acknowledged it with silence.

Unwilling to revisit the painful past of his parents' marriage, Ethan pulled a hand through his hair and sighed. "Go on," he coaxed. "Tell me the rest of it."

"Sondra worked on me for two years. Little changes here, a new way of looking at things there. I was actually beginning to see a future for myself." He dropped his head. It suddenly seemed as though the weight of the world was on his shoulders. "And then some drunken bum broadsided her as he was running a red light. By the time I got to the hospital, there wasn't anything they could do. I was holding her hand, just waiting. Crying. Cursing God like I used to."

Remembering how frightened he had been for Cassie after her accident, Ethan could imagine the devastation his father must have felt.

Hugh drew a deep breath. "But then, just as clear as a bell, Sondra looks up to me and says, 'Don't you dare throw away what we've accomplished together. I'm counting on you, Hugh Rafferty.' Then she just…slipped away."

"And you've been sober ever since."

"Nope." Hugh rubbed his eyes as if he was tired, though Ethan suspected the memory of Sondra's death had gotten to him. His father gave him a weak smile. "Went right out and got stinking drunk. When I woke up the next day, I felt like I'd been pounded into the mud. I remembered what that was like, and realized how good it felt to be clearheaded when I was off the booze. Plus, I figured if Sondra cared enough about me to get me shaped up, who was I to throw all her hard work away? So I turned my back on my old vices, and the new ones I've acquired since then haven't been near as bad."

Ethan stared at his father. The silence stretched out, but it was not uneasy.

The lines in Hugh's face looked deep enough to have been carved with a knife, but he said robustly, "That's my tale, and I'm sticking to it. I'm taking it day by day, sometimes hour by hour, but I think Sondra would be proud of me. So what do *you* say?"

"I say, do you think you could manage not to get into any more disagreements while you're in town? I have enough to take care of without making sure you stay in one piece."

"Why, son," Hugh said in a playfully shocked tone. "Are you saying you care what happens to me?"

Punching his pillow, Ethan sighed and fixed him with the hardest look he had in his arsenal. "I need good help, and so far, you're it. But I don't have insurance to cover you getting the crap beat out of you. So keep it under control, or I *will* kick your ass back to Louisiana, no matter how much Sondra was able to accomplish with you. Got it?"

"Got it."

They exchanged narrow, tight smiles. And yet their eyes met in a long look of complete understanding. "Good. Now go to sleep."

CHAPTER THIRTEEN

BY THE TIME THE WEEKEND rolled around, Ethan was in a better mood than he had been in a while. A better mood than he'd have thought possible, considering the fact that his son was having fun camping out in the wilderness with his adopted father while *he* was faced with the grim prospect of having to talk to a shrink sometime soon. Hell, that ought to make his skin crawl like nails on a chalkboard.

But a promise was a promise. He'd go. If Donny needed the help, then so be it.

Besides, agreeing to Cassie's request had certainly helped bring down some of the walls between them. Perhaps not all of them, and not for good, but enough that he felt they were making progress.

He just wished he could find a legitimate way to be with her again. Work had swallowed him whole since their dinner a few nights ago, and he hadn't seen her since.

Right now, construction on the property took up most of his time. He and Quintin were up to their ears in paperwork, decisions and preparation. A few more day laborers had been hired. Hugh had been on his best behavior, thank God, and Ethan had to admit the man was pulling his weight. The three of them worked sunup to sundown, barely stopping for a quick meal, and fell into bed exhausted every night, where they slept like the dead.

But on Saturday morning, right in the middle of digging postholes for a corral, Ethan looked up and saw a rider emerge from the woods bordering the property. He recognized Cassie coming toward him on the back of the bay mare.

Considering her past, it surprised him to see her on a horse. She rode well, with a good seat and erect posture, and with no insecurity in spite of her damaged leg.

He leaned against his hole digger, wiping sweat from his brow with the back of his sleeve as he waited for her to reach him. When she did, he smiled. She offered one in return, though it was tentative. He couldn't help noting that it didn't hold anything resembling the lustful enthusiasm she had exhibited in the hotel alcove the other night.

Still, the pleasure in seeing her again caused his heart to miss a couple of beats.

He laid his hand along the mare's reins, holding it in place. Cassie didn't get down from the saddle. "Out making neighborly visits?" he asked.

"Just thought I'd come over to see how you were doing."

"I would have expected you to drive the truck."

"Riding over gave me time to think. And Sheba needed the exercise." She used a gloved hand to pat the bay's sleek neck. Then she surveyed the property briefly. "So. How is it going?"

Ethan brought her up-to-date. He pointed out the shells of cabins being built in a row, the big barn still in its early stages of construction, and half a dozen smaller projects taking shape.

Finally, he indicated the far corner of the property with a lift of his chin. "Do you want me to tell you all about the well they're drilling over there?" He let his mouth form a tempting slant of lecherous intent. "Or would you rather hear about how much I've missed seeing you?"

"I don't know… That well looks pretty fascinating."

"So do you." He extended a hand to help her dismount. "Want to come down and stay awhile?"

"I can't," she said with a grimace. "I have the vet coming out to deworm calves at one."

He laughed. His hand fell to her jeans-covered leg, which was only an inch or two from his mouth. He wished suddenly she was bare-legged. "I love it when you talk dirty," he said as he planted a kiss directly on her knee.

"You're incorrigible," she told him. He placed his hand on her thigh, and she slapped it away. "Behave, damn it, or I'll let Sheba take a bite out of you. She's a nipper."

He straightened, suddenly all business. "I'm at your command."

"Oh, if only that were true," she retorted in a dry tone. "Actually…" She looked away as though unsure of herself, and when she spoke, her tone was much more serious. "Umm, I did have a specific reason for coming over."

"Something wrong? Josh and Donny still having fun in the great outdoors?"

"They're fine. I got a call from Josh this morning. He says they're having a great time. They've caught lots of fish, which I, unfortunately, will have to find new ways to cook."

"Wonderful. Any problems with Donny?"

"He's behaving himself lately."

"Probably because he knows you and Josh will be on him if he doesn't."

"Actually, I came over to ask you if you'd like to meet me in town tonight. There's a public concert at Riverfront Park, and I thought…I thought it might be fun. The house feels very empty without Donny around, even when he's at his worst."

Ethan narrowed his eyes. Not in suspicion, really—more like surprise. "You're asking me out on a date?"

"Not exactly a date," she replied quickly. He watched her neck turn pink, then a lovely shade of red. "Just to listen to some music, and enjoy the night. It's an open-air auditorium, and sometimes the sky puts on quite a show."

"I thought it was supposed to rain tonight."

"Only a thirty percent chance. Don't be such a gloom-and-doomer."

"You and me? No one else?"

"Yes. Just the two of us."

"It's not opera, is it?"

"No. If you don't want to go, that's all right—"

"No, I'll go. Sounds like fun. When do you want me to pick you up?"

"Can you meet me there? I'm on the committee and it's my turn to help set up."

"Are you fishing for me to come early? Need some muscle to move stuff?"

She met his glittering gaze head-on. "I am not fishing."

"You sure?"

"Come or don't come," she said with a shrug. "It's up to you. It starts at seven. I'll be in the back row."

Before he could say another word, she kicked Sheba into movement, and galloped away. The last he saw of her, she was disappearing back into the woods that led to the Flying M.

"Oh, I'll come," Ethan said softly. He smiled. "Even if it's opera, I'll come."

THE NECHES RIVER RAN in a slow-moving, winding current past Beaumont, then finally flowed into Sabine Lake and the Mississippi. It wasn't a particularly attractive body of water, but it cooled off the city in the worst of summers, and made a nice focal point for the revitalization of downtown Beaumont that had started a few years ago.

Cassie was especially fond of Riverfront Park, mostly because she'd persuaded the city fathers to give her a major role in its recovery from the last recession. Over the years, gardening had become a passion for her. Her willingness to work and enthusiasm for the project had impressed the board and far outweighed the business résumés of landscaping companies, who were too expensive and not true "Beaumonters."

The annual River Festival was held here, along with several other events throughout the year, so Cassie found herself at the park a lot. Every time she came—even if it was only to sit on one of the riverfront benches and enjoy the weather—she felt refreshed and inexplicably young at heart.

She was feeling that way right now, though she knew it had little to do with the soft breeze off the river or the scent of roses from the nearby garden.

A date with Ethan. That was what had her pulse racing.

She'd spent more than an hour getting ready for this evening, though she'd still ended up wearing nothing more elaborate than black jeans and a crisp, emerald-green blouse that complemented her hair. She'd taken special care with her makeup and even dabbed on a little perfume—not wiping it away this time.

So yes, she'd told Ethan this wasn't a date, but from her perspective, it sure looked like one, and she didn't care. She didn't want to come to her senses. She was way beyond that now, anyway.

When they'd had dinner the other night, she'd discovered that she could let herself enjoy time spent with him. Even when they disagreed, it didn't have to get nasty or difficult. Donny was *their* son, and she'd begun to think that maybe they could move beyond an either/or type of future. Maybe there really would be a way to make everyone happy. As long as they continued to work toward that goal, Ethan's agreement about Dr. Parker, the psychologist, gave her hope for that.

Not that she expected everything to go smoothly from here on. She'd yet to hear exactly what Ethan would consider a "fair" custody arrangement once Donny was told. And not that she ever imagined they could build a real relationship again. Well, she might have conjured one up in her fantasies, but that didn't count.

Still, when she'd ended up in Ethan's arms that night, she couldn't help but feel as though she were suddenly hovering at the edge of an old dream, a fragment of a life she had not been entirely able to leave behind. It had left her amazed. Joyful. And so scared that she'd been desperate to get away from him before she could do something completely stupid.

But maybe she wasn't very bright, after all, because here she was, sitting in the back row of the park's open-air amphitheater, waiting for Ethan to show up. *Oh, Cassie,* she thought. *You do know how to complicate things.*

The program scheduled for tonight was a small orchestra from Houston. The concert wouldn't start until seven-thirty and it was only six now. That didn't matter. Beaumonters loved these kinds of events and often showed up early to eat food packed in picnic baskets, play with their kids, read or just soak up the atmosphere. Cassie hadn't been able to resist arriving early to join them and people-watch.

Movement at the corner of her eye made her turn her head. She was surprised to see Ethan coming toward her along the wide cement rows, paper bag in one hand, backpack in the other.

The mere sight of him made her feel both hot and cold, restless and content.

"You're early," she said as he settled beside her on the step.

"So are you. Guess we were both anxious to see one another again."

She didn't offer him a response. Instead, she pointed toward the bag. "What's in there?"

"I did my homework. Turns out the hotel can put together a nice picnic dinner for guests. Simple, but elegant." He held up the backpack. "In here I have a blanket so we don't have to sit on the bare concrete, a flashlight, extra water and rain gear." He lifted his eyebrows. "In case you were wrong about that thirty percent chance of showers."

"You're very thorough. I'm surprised."

Ethan began spreading out the blanket. So far they had the back row completely to themselves. "Why? Because I used to be such a fly-by-the-seat-of-your-pants kind of guy? I still am. But over the years I've gotten better about planning." His lips curved suggestively. "Especially if it's something important."

Cassie was saved from having to reply when he offered his left hand to entice her onto the blanket. Excitement zipped through her as his fingers clasped hers, strength against softness. She wanted him to hold her hand this way forever. A simple touch. How silly.

When they were seated side by side, Ethan scanned the area—the people already having fun, the river moving slowly under the bridge, the new spring grass that looked so bright and soft.

"Very pretty," he said at last. "You said you have something to do with this place?"

"There are separate committees that help take care of every park in the city. Part of our beautification project. We don't do the heavy stuff, of course, but we plan activities, help the landscape designers. There are one hundred and sixty-seven trees in this park, and I've nurtured every one of them. Those begonias over there?" She pointed, then raised her hands and wiggled her fingers. "Believe it or not, I planted them."

"I'm impressed. I never realized you were so interested in nature."

"I've developed an interest over the years," she replied off-handedly.

"I wish I could have been here," he said, suddenly

sounding serious. He gave her a simple, straightforward glance. "To see you grow into the woman you are today."

It didn't need to be said, but they both knew how different things might have turned out if he'd stayed. But that was the past, and right now, under Ethan's gaze, she didn't want to think about it. Her cheeks felt so flushed she thought she might spontaneously combust at any moment.

For diversion, she tapped the paper bag. "Why don't we eat?"

He began spreading out the banquet the hotel had prepared. *Simple* and *elegant* were the right words, she thought, as he pulled out wine and real glasses, snowy cloth napkins, a baguette, cheeses, meat, fruit and rich-looking chocolate truffles.

"All we're missing is the French countryside," she said.

They ate and chatted and laughed. Neither one of them talked about Donny much. It seemed as though they were both determined to put aside any discussion that might spoil the mood.

More people arrived. The sunset tinted the park gold and pink, making everything look like an enchanted fairyland. Two rows down from them, a teenaged couple seemed absorbed in finding each other's tonsils. Cassie thought it a little embarrassing. Ethan seemed to find their out-of-control hormones amusing.

He bent close to say softly, "Right out of *Romeo and Juliet.*"

Cassie nodded. "If Romeo had had a nose ring and Juliet had a tattoo."

"Reminds me of us," he said with a laugh.

She gave him a scandalized look. "It most certainly does not. We never acted that way."

"I think we must have, or there would be no Donny."

"I mean, we never behaved that way in public."

"That's because we were never able to *be* in public together."

She gave him a weak smile. That was certainly true. Even before her father's horrible rant that night in the hospital emergency room, they'd both known that Mac McGuire would never have considered Ethan good enough for her. The whole idea of eloping had come from that knowledge.

Cassie grimaced, thinking how much she had loved her father, but regretting how stubbornly feudal he could be at times. She was nibbling a piece of crusty bread slathered with butter when a sudden thought occurred to her. She straightened, making eye contact with Ethan.

"I want to ask you something. We both know what my father thought, but twice now I've gotten the impression that you think I agreed with him. That somehow you weren't good enough. But you know that isn't true, don't you? If I'd thought that, I'd never have agreed to elope."

Ethan carefully set down his wineglass. He tried to smile at her, but didn't quite succeed. "Do you really want to spoil a nice evening?"

"I don't see why the evening has to change just because there's a little truth between us."

"All right. I'll tell you…"

"Truthfully."

"Truthfully," he repeated with a rueful glance. Then he sighed heavily. "Your father told me flat out that I was no damned good for you, that I was only after your money. You may not have necessarily believed that part, but I think the night of the accident you realized just how different things were going to be if we got married—"

"Things *were* going to be different. They were going to be wonderful."

He gave her a skeptical look. "C'mon, Cass. We've agreed to speak the truth. I told you long ago the kind of stock I come from, and you got a taste of it yourself the other night in that bar. You don't want my dad around Donny. Hell, if you're going to be honest, you'll admit you don't even think *I'm* good enough. Not to be his father."

She was so shocked that it took her a long moment to absorb what he'd said, much less think of a reply. Finally, she shook her head. "I don't know where you're getting this. Yes, your dad seems rough around the edges, but from the way you used to describe him, I was expecting a lot worse. And I never said you weren't fit to be a father. I only think you don't know how to be one. As for whether or not you were good enough for me…" She glanced away for a moment, unsure how to proceed.

"You said I wasn't."

She swung around to face him again. "When?"

"That night at the hospital. Before you went into surgery you told me we were too different. That you'd realized you didn't want the life I could give you and that I'd never fit into yours. Pretty specific, I'd say."

"Ethan…"

"It's all right," he told her. "I came to terms with it a long time ago."

When she just continued to stare at him, he went on to tell her about the time he'd come back to the Flying

M, determined to face her. Her father, too. How he'd seen her, but had been unable to approach because his pride just wouldn't let him. No one should have to beg to be loved.

It grew quiet between them. So quiet that the scrape of Ethan's shoe against the gritty concrete made Cassie want to cover her ears, but she couldn't because she was stunned into stillness. Her eyes were fixed on the golden thread of the river, watching the sluggish current slip under the bridge.

She felt Ethan's hand cover hers. "Don't think about it. That was light-years ago, and we were both too young to handle—"

"I know how I would have handled it," she interrupted vehemently, turning to face him. "If I'd known you'd come back to the ranch, I would have jumped into your arms no matter what Dad tried to do to stop me. I was so unhappy without you."

Ethan gave her a small smile. "That isn't the impression you left me with at the hospital," he said softly.

"I hardly remember what I said, but I thought I was going to lose my leg. I thought I'd be crippled, or in a wheelchair for the rest of my life. I couldn't do that to you. Not after we'd talked so much about seeing the world together."

He looked shocked. It was his turn to look surprised. "How could you have made that decision for the both of us? Do you really think that would have mattered to me? I've seen the world, and believe me, it loses a lot of appeal when there's no one to share it with."

Cassie drew a breath. "I'm sorry. I just couldn't think clearly at the time. I thought I knew what I had to do."

"God, Cass. You couldn't have been more wrong."

Seeing her stricken look, Ethan stroked her arm consolingly. "Well, it's done. And as I said, we were both too young." He tapped her glass. "Drink your wine. You look pale."

She did as he suggested, mostly because she was still at a loss for words. She polished off the Chablis and cleared her throat, wishing she'd never brought up their past.

Luckily, the visiting orchestra took the stage at that point, and she could pretend to be fascinated by the process of setup and practice. Night began to settle around them, sweet and cool, but Cassie's face still felt flushed, and a lump seemed to block her windpipe, making it difficult to breathe.

Beside her, Ethan remained quiet, but not distant. He seemed prepared to enjoy the evening, as though conversation between them had gone no deeper than a discussion of the weather.

Along the river, the old-time lamppost lights came on. Mist wrapped around them like schools of silvery fish. The air carried a velvety mildness. The orchestra knew how to please a crowd, bringing everyone to their feet with a rousing rendition of the national anthem.

When Cassie and Ethan settled back on the blanket, he pulled her to his side, feeling for her hand again in the dark. Cassie did not resist. She relaxed against him. His warmth enveloped her like silken bonds stronger than iron.

She tried to give herself over to the music. She wanted to drift away to the melodic sounds of Mozart and Beethoven. She was all through with the world for the moment and the orchestra was certainly skilled enough to guarantee that.

But somehow it didn't work.

Everything about the evening was so beautiful, so perfect. Pressed against Ethan, Cassie realized that it was possible for your spirit to rise and fall simultaneously. She felt as though her insides had been washed away and regret was rising in her like a wave. She was suffocating, drowning beneath the surprises and shocks of what Ethan had just told her.

All those years ago, he had come back for her.

CHAPTER FOURTEEN

COULD IT REALLY BE TRUE?

So hard to believe. All those years ago, Ethan had wanted to fight for her.

Cassie wished she could rush back through the years and change everything, even knowing the impossibility of such a hope.

Closing her eyes, she tried to concentrate on the music. The orchestra swept into "Bist Du Bei Mir" now, one of her favorites. "Be Thou with Me." The dark, deep notes of the cello glided and moaned with an almost human need. Tears gathered at the back of Cassie's eyes, blurring her vision.

By the time the musicians struck the last chord of the evening's performance, her control was teetering. Her nerve endings hummed. Along with the rest of the crowd, she and Ethan rose, offering applause and shouts of approval. He dipped his head to catch her ear over the noise.

"I once heard the London Symphony perform. I think Houston has them beat," he said. "And I'll bet they make better chili, too."

She tried to laugh lightly at that comment, but failed. She couldn't look at him. It felt as though every thought in her head would be there in her features, and she couldn't let him know just how much her resolve had been shaken. She needed time to sort through it all, to let control and common sense take hold once more. She had to reject the notion that Ethan had bewitched her lonely heart into yearnings it had not felt for years.

The audience began to disperse, though a few people stayed where they were, enjoying the night air. Romeo and Juliet were back at it, necking and cuddling close. Cassie certainly didn't want to spend more time watching them. She bent to slip items back into the paper bag, while Ethan folded the blanket, placed it over his arm and hefted the backpack.

"Something wrong?" he asked, as Cassie finished gathering what was left of their picnic spread.

She flashed him an overbright smile. "Nothing." Then, because he eyed her with such intensity, she motioned skyward. "I just don't want to get caught in the rain. Looks like you were right, after all."

He frowned and glanced up. The sky was dark, and heat lightning flashed in the distance, but no one seemed in a hurry. Many couples had begun a slow, leg-stretching ramble along the walkway that led out of the park.

Cassie navigated the tiered exit. In spite of some stiffness in her bad leg, she took the steps two at a time, as though demons were after her. Ethan caught up with her and took her elbow.

"Slow down," he told her. "You're going to fall."

Too late, she wanted to shout. *I fell a long time ago, and I'm in trouble here.*

As she reached the wide pathway, the wind picked up, sending strands of hair whipping across her face. Overhead, tree branches suddenly looked as if they were wrestling with one another. Fat, cold drops of rain began to fall.

People squealed and made a laughing run for cover. Ethan grabbed Cassie's hand, intent on leading her to the nearest building overhang. It seemed a ridiculously long way away; they'd be soaked by the time they reached it.

She pulled against his grasp. "I know someplace closer," she told him over the sound of pelting rain.

Yanking him along, she swung off the path and ran across the grass. It felt spongy, giving beneath her shoes, but she kept going until they reached the gardener's shack. Cassie, who had been part of too many projects to count, knew just where to find the hidden key.

She rammed it into the padlock and pushed against the door. They stumbled inside the darkened room as if they'd been blown there, while rain continued to drum against the tin roof.

They were both breathing hard. Eerie light came in from the only window, but it was pouring so hard that no sense could be made of the scene outside. Ethan immediately began searching along the wall for the light switch.

"Don't," she said, still gasping for air. Water dripped down her cheek. "No one can know we're in here."

"Why? Do we have something to hide?"

Her eyes hadn't fully adjusted to the darkness yet, but she could just make him out—a tall, silvery shadow standing only a few feet from her. She stared at him hard, wanting to believe that she glimpsed in his face what she was feeling inside—the inevitability of this moment, the endless, burning grip of desire that had built and built and built within her….

In the next instant, Cassie moved across the distance that separated them. She was with him. They were alone.

An explosive, all-consuming flare of need took over, passion so sharp it was like daggers against her nerve endings. She wouldn't be able to take another breath if she couldn't touch him, taste him, wrap herself around him as if he were her only lifeline.

"Cassie—"

She caught his words with a kiss. A free, abandoned, frighteningly natural act. She had been wanting this all evening. She had been wanting it for thirteen years, if she was perfectly honest with herself.

She pushed against him. In a vast burst of lightning, she saw his eyes flash with blue longing, and she lifted her hands to lay them on either side of his face. His mouth parted further, and their sleek, seeking tongues met and tangled. His eyelashes against her cheek felt like a small animal's heartbeat. A hard shiver that had nothing to do with her rain-soaked body ran the length of her spine.

"You're cold," he said in a quiet voice, so near and intimate.

"No. Burning." She pressed closer, trying to feel every inch of him through the clinging wetness of their clothes. "I want you." She nibbled at his lips. "I want you inside me."

He needed no further invitation. His mouth took hers again and again as he stripped her blouse and jeans from her body, though she really didn't know how it happened so quickly or where Ethan's own clothes went. He laid her down, and she found the warmth and softness of the blanket he'd carried suddenly under her. How had he managed to do that and yet never turn her loose?

"Wait," he told her, reaching for his jeans. When his hand appeared again, she glimpsed a square packet in his palm. "Would you be annoyed if I told you I came prepared?" he asked. "Just in case."

"I think you're brilliant." She smiled at him. "But hurry."

She watched as he took care of protecting her. It seemed to take forever, but finally, the hesitant first touch of his hand played against her breast. A half-suppressed moan filled her throat as, featherlight, his fingers brushed over her nipple. She arched under him.

Pale, watery light poured from the high, square window of the shed to form a veil of woven silver over Ethan's body. It caught and held the symmetry of his cheekbones, his shoulders, the curve of his hips as he rose, then settled against her. Even after all these years, what she glimpsed of him was so perfect.

She drew a sharp little breath and stiffened as his hand came under the knee of her bad leg, caressing the flesh as he pulled upward. "Ethan, don't…"

He stilled immediately, frowning down at her. "What is it, sweetheart? Have I hurt you?"

"No. It's just…it's just that my body isn't the way it used to be. I'm…"

"Don't be embarrassed." He bent his head and brushed her mouth with his. The touch was brief and light, but sufficient enough to reassure Cassie that desire still smoldered just beneath the surface. "When I fell in love with you, it wasn't because of your legs or your hair—" he gently rubbed one nipple "—or these beauti-ful breasts."

His candor pleased and amused her. "Really?" she challenged. "You're saying you'd have made love to me if I'd been as ugly as a two-headed calf?"

His teeth flashed white in the shadows. "Yes, I would have. But very carefully." He kissed her deeply. "Now stop fretting and let me show you what we've missed."

He ran his hand slowly along her scarred thigh. She stiffened more at first, but he didn't stop, and soon the tightened muscles began to relax. Vaguely, she wondered if her scars repulsed him. Had he lied to protect her feelings? Then she ceased to care about anything except the endless sensations swarming over and inside her body.

Spreading her fingers, she ran her hands up the softly fleeced muscles of his bare chest, then drew him close again. They slid against one another with maximum contact, and while the pressure of his hips on her inner thighs seemed so determined and focused, his touch was a murmur on her flesh. She felt as though she were melting into the stroke of his fingers. *Oh, yes. Lovely.* His body fit so well with hers that after a while she forgot the feeling of separation entirely.

He eased her legs apart, touching her so that she gasped at the sudden, bright flare of need. And then, somehow, he was inside her. Full and hard.

The breath quickened in her throat and in his. She heard his swift intake of air. He whispered her name softly over and over, as though for his own pleasure. His voice sank into her senses.

"Ethan…" His name escaped her lips in a rough, convulsive whisper, begging for release. And Cassie knew he would be there to offer it.

"It's all right." As though holding on to the thinnest filament of control, he brought his hands to her hair, pushing it away from her forehead so that he could find her face.

His hold on her was so gentle, and yet electric. They

still…fit. The contours, the grooves of their bodies needed no adjusting, and the years began to drift away. He thrust against her, and then out, every muscle moving in a flawless synchronicity of confidence.

It was a cycle that didn't seem to have an end, and she loved it. Before, she had succumbed to a warm tide of pleasure. But now, now his movements made her heart slip into overdrive, made something flood up from within her and overwhelm her. She clutched him closer, deeper, welcoming him as a parched blossom seeks restorative rain.

He followed her, trembling and tense. His low cry was hoarse and harsh, and slightly surprised, as though the power of what they shared shocked him, too. Then he fell against her with a long shudder as passion passed through him one last time.

With a long sigh Ethan slid beside her and gathered her close. They were sated, complete and almost spell-bound with shared delight. His arm lay stretched under her head. She could feel his fingers stroking the sweat-dampened hair along her temple. The rhythmic move-ment sent delicious, enveloping bliss through her body. She thought she could have closed her eyes right then and slept for a week. It felt good, to be so sleepy in his arms.

They were silent for a long time. So long that Cassie wondered if she had nodded off for a few moments. When she turned her head, Ethan was lying on his side, watching her while he played with her hair. A smile flirted with his lips.

"What do you see when you look at me?" His voice, though quiet, was startling in the silence.

She stretched a fingertip and lightly stroked his

bottom lip. "I see a second chance," she whispered, and by the look on his face she knew her words had pleased him.

"Your hair usually has all the colors of fire," he said. "But in this light, it's like liquid silver."

"It's this romantic atmosphere," she replied, glancing around the darkened shed full of wheelbarrows, weed-cutters and the wicked shadows of a dozen different lawn tools.

"We should come here more often."

She laughed out loud, then suddenly had to stop because she caught herself in the midst of a shockingly erotic daydream. She felt her heart tumbling. And this strange sensation, this bubbling in her breast? She remembered it. Happiness.

Oh, God. Really, Cassie? A toolshed?

Though she wasn't entirely comfortable about how this had happened, she had no sense of shame about it, either. She turned her head into his chest, unable to keep from laughing. She couldn't seem to help herself at all, around Ethan.

As though alarmed, he came up on one elbow, trying to coax her to look at him. "Cassie, what is it? Please. Don't cry."

She let him see her smile. He gave her a frown of mock distress. "What's so funny? If it's my performance you're laughing about, I'll admit it's been a while, but I thought I held up my end pretty well."

She shook her head, denying any complaint. "You were wonderful. It's just… When we were eighteen, this would have seemed like our own private Eden. But now that I'm in my thirties, it's hard to believe I've just had sex in a toolshed."

"It's a very nice toolshed. And I'd just like to remind you that you started it. I felt it all evening—the tension inside you, begging for release."

"I did start it, didn't I? God, I thought that wild girl was long gone."

"Evidently not." He leaned over to touch his lips to hers. "Welcome back. I missed you."

"I've missed you, too." She stared up into the shed's rafters, trying to find the words to tell him what she felt. So obvious to her now, and yet so hard to admit. She had fallen in love with him thirteen years ago, and nothing had changed. She loved him still.

She propped her hand under her head so she could face him, see him better. "Tonight, everything between us seemed to be…tipping." She shook her head, disappointed that she couldn't find a better way to say it. "I can't explain it, really. But tonight, everything feels dangerous because of you, and at the same time everything feels dangerous except right where you are."

He reached out to tweak one of her dangling curls. "There's no danger in being with me. You're a grown woman now, free to be with anyone you want." His knuckles moved to her lips, to brush against the lush fullness of her mouth. "Don't you know how much I want you?"

Want, not love. Take it easy, Cassie. Keep it light until you know more about what he's thinking.

She ran a finger across his bare collarbone, until he caught it and placed a kiss on the tip. "I think you just showed me how much," she said with a playful grin. "But I might need a second demonstration."

"My pleasure." He grabbed her up, and when she made a feeble attempt to slip out from under him, he pushed her against the blanket. They kissed and nuzzled each other until they were both gasping. When Ethan slid on top of her, she looked at him in wide-eyed delight.

"Umm…are you sure we can do this so soon? I mean, don't you have to wait or something…?"

"Let me worry about that," he said, and in no time, he was coaxing her body to respond to him in ways she would never have thought possible. With his labored, uneven breath whispering in her ear, Cassie rose to meet him, inhaling his scent and warmth. His hands were so deft, so talented, and in no time, under his skilled touch her body began to unravel like lace again, bringing her to the brink.

He stopped suddenly, lying over her. Still. Their gazes met and clung. Ethan didn't move, didn't move—she lifted questioning eyes and realized that he was making sure she could take all of him again without pain—and then he did move. Slowly, caressingly, building pleasure upon pleasure until their bodies merged and Cassie felt as if she were soaring weightless. Free.

Some time later, she lay against him once more, her head pillowed on his arm. Her body felt heavy and fluid, and she knew that if she could see her face, her lips would be tinted as deep as a summer rose from Ethan's kisses. Her lover was tempestuous, treating her more like the seductress she'd secretly yearned to become than the modest, practical lady her father had tried so hard to rear.

Cassie's smile grew dreamy as she thought about what they'd done here.

The rain had stopped. The moon was high in the window, washing the shed with white light. As she moved, her opal ring caught a moonbeam, flashing a brilliant blue-and-green fire.

Ethan took her hand, examining the ring. "Where did you get this?" he asked softly.

"It's Donny's birthstone."

"Was it a gift?"

"Yes." She considered leaving it at that, but didn't want to have any more secrets between them. "From Josh. After Donny was born."

Ethan contemplated the simple band, twisting it a little on her finger to catch more light. She could only guess his thoughts. She wondered if he could sense how tense she was as he examined the ring.

His gaze came to hers slowly. "Will you tell me about your marriage to Josh?" he asked softly. "What it was really like."

"Does it matter?"

"It matters to me."

Cassie had to pause to catch her breath. Ethan lifted her hand to his lips. His fingers were reassuringly strong, his palm warm and comforting against hers. It was an uncomplicated gesture of understanding about how difficult it was to talk about her marriage to Josh. One she suspected he hadn't planned.

She felt her mouth quirk, but not with humor. "We both worked hard at it for many years," she told him in a low voice. "I knew Josh was in love with me, and I thought I could learn to love him back. We tried to make it real and satisfying. Josh is a good man, a great father to Donny. Any woman should consider herself lucky to have him."

"But…?"

"But that special spark was just never there," Cassie

admitted. She plunged ahead as though some inner dam had just broken. "We were a couple, but not in any real sense of the word. We fooled ourselves for a long time, but last year we just couldn't do it anymore."

"Why?"

"Josh cheated on me. A one-time fling with a woman we met at a horse auction in San Antonio."

She felt Ethan tense. He still held her hand, and now he turned it to press a kiss into her palm, arousing sensations that spread through her body until it felt too warm. "I'm sorry," he said. "You had a lot of love to give, and you deserved better than that."

"I'm not sure I did," Cassie said. "I'd been sensing Josh's unhappiness for months, but I never really tried to fix things. We still had a great friendship, and a mutual love for Donny, but that's all. It wasn't enough for either of us. I couldn't really blame him."

"Still, it must have been a very difficult decision."

"Only as far as Donny was concerned. Neither of us wanted him to be hurt. When we sat down and confronted our marriage, we were both so relieved to have the truth out there in the open. It got easier after that."

Ethan leaned forward and brushed her mouth lightly with his. "So what are you wanting out of life now?"

You, she longed to say. *I want to stay right here in your arms, where I feel safe, cocooned.* But that kind of confession couldn't come. Her voice was very calm, her expression composed as she gave him a friendly enough smile. "I want Donny to be happy."

Ethan frowned. "I'm not talking about Donny. I'm talking about you."

"I don't know what I want. He's been my whole life for so long."

"Maybe you should give your own future some thought now."

Ethan smiled at her expectantly, but she couldn't help wondering what was really behind the shadowed eyes and the masculine planes of his face. What would he say if she told him that she loved him, that she was already desperate with desire again? That her flesh was on fire for him?

As it turned out, she said none of those things. Nor anything else. Ethan had locked the shed door behind them, but at that moment it rattled. Cassie let out a startled gasp as Ethan pressed a finger to his lips.

The door shook as someone tried the lock again and again. Then they both heard laughter, high giggles and low calls for silence.

Ethan lips found Cassie's ear. "Kids, probably. Don't move."

Her heart pounded as they waited. Whatever mischief the intruders had in mind they were quick to give up. A few more annoyed attempts at the latch and then silence returned. Ethan got to his feet—he seemed completely unbothered by his nakedness—and went to the window. After a moment, he turned back to her, a grin on his face.

"Two boys, two girls," he confirmed. "They probably heard what a great make-out place this is."

Cassie rose, pulling the blanket around her as she searched for her clothes. "Get dressed," she said in a whisper. "We have to go."

"Why?"

"Because the last thing I want is to be caught naked in a toolshed with the new guy in town."

"All right. Let's go back to my hotel room. I have a great bed."

"I can't."

"Why not?"

"Because a single act of insanity is all I can handle for one day," she said, hoping she didn't have a full-blown anxiety attack before she could find her missing jeans. "And this was it."

CHAPTER FIFTEEN

TWO DAYS LATER, Ethan stood at the Horse Sense campsite, pouring coffee into a plastic foam cup. The brew looked like Mississippi mud, which told him his father must have made it. But instead of tossing it, he downed the entire cup, then a second. He needed something strong to keep him going these days.

It had been too long since he'd seen Cassie, and he was pretty sure he was going mad. After she'd refused to come back to his hotel room on Saturday night, she'd dropped him off at the hotel lobby. He had kissed her just before midnight, then watched her taillights recede into the misty darkness, away from him. Back to her old life.

Sometimes, during the lonely hours when he was supposed to be sleeping but wasn't, he could almost believe that the time in the toolshed had never happened. What they had shared, the culmination of so many years of longing, seemed the stuff of fantasies, of dreams. Had he actually held Cassie in his arms again? Had they really made love?

Love. Yeah, that was the right word. He still loved her. Irrational, wrong, stupid, whatever. He still loved her. Deep in his soul, when he was really honest with himself, he knew he'd probably never *stopped* loving her.

He couldn't think about anything else. About how maybe it was possible to start again, to have a new chance, get it right this time. He understood that they were no longer the people they had been, neither of them. But all he needed was one more opportunity. And if he got it, he would never let it slip away again. He would take better care of her heart than he did his own.

Could she trust him? Would she even believe him?

He'd heard nothing from her since that night. He knew that Josh and Donny had returned from their camping trip. It was possible she'd been too caught up with family matters to give him much thought. The idea chafed, but it was better than thinking that she now regretted what they'd shared, and was already putting it behind her.

"Insanity," she'd called it. He supposed that was one way of looking at it. But if that was all they could ever have between them, he'd take it.

Realizing he'd been daydreaming too long, Ethan headed back to the corral, where his father was putting Donny through his paces with Cochise. The kid had shown up bright and early this morning, looking determined to have a lesson before the men had to start the real work of getting Sense up and running.

Ethan joined Quintin at the rail and handed him a cup of coffee. "How's he doing?"

Quintin took a sip from his cup. "Damn, this coffee's strong enough to melt iron," he said with a grimace. "Who? The kid or Cochise?"

"Both."

"Cochise showed up tense, but Hugh rubbed most of it out of him. Donny's uptight this morning, too. Had a fight with his mother over breakfast. Something about seeing a psychologist."

So Cassie had finally addressed that decision with the boy. That had to have been difficult. "He's not the only one who doesn't want to do it," Ethan muttered.

In the corral, Donny cantered Cochise in a tight circle. The palomino clearly didn't like the workout. He gave a half buck, nearly unseating Donny. Hugh, guiding them with a lunge line, yelled out, "Pay attention, boy! I said cue him up."

"Give me a chance!" Donny called back in annoyance.

Ethan glanced at Quintin. "Think we should skip the lesson today? He's in a mood."

Quintin gave him a sideways glance coupled with a grin. "Getting to know your son well enough to determine that, huh? Good job, Dad."

"Doesn't take much to recognize a surly teenager when you see one," Ethan replied, though he smiled a little at the idea that maybe he wasn't quite as clueless when it came to kids as he'd thought.

"Things have been going so well, I think we should keep it up. Cochise needs to knock off that bucking, and if Donny gets dumped, it won't hurt him."

"That's my son you're talking about."

Quintin just laughed.

The workout in the ring picked up pace. Hugh was pushing Cochise hard now, forcing the animal to realize that if he didn't follow Donny's commands, the penalty would be more work. Both boy and horse were sweating under the morning sun, but the set of Donny's jaw suggested he was resolved to ride out the hard parts.

Ethan had to admit that his father was great at this. There wasn't a single thing he himself would have done differently. Since the night they'd talked in the hotel room, the two men seemed to have reached a better understanding of one another. No close relationship had developed, but if Ethan could believe he actually stood a chance at having Cassie in his life again, he was willing to entertain the possibility that he and his father could eventually come to terms.

Quintin and Ethan turned as they heard a vehicle approaching. A Flying M truck pulled into the property, and Ethan saw Cassie behind the wheel. Just glimpsing her he got that cool, heart-racing feeling in his chest. The day suddenly looked brighter.

He heard Quintin laugh. "Man, you ought to see your face," his partner said. "Could you be any more obvious?"

Ethan didn't look at him; he couldn't take his eyes off Cassie. But he grinned. "Shut up, Quint. Nobody asked you."

Cassie had parked and gotten out of the truck. She was smiling as she approached, and offered a cheery flutter of one hand in greeting.

Definitely a good sign, right? Ethan began to shorten the distance that separated them. He noticed that her hair was down, shiny and framing her face like a shimmery red cloud. Instantly, he couldn't wait to crush it in his hands and inhale the scent of flowers he knew he'd find there. She'd be a dream to wake up next to every morning. Warm and soft and just a little bit grumpy.

They had nearly reached one another when Cassie stopped, her gaze flicking to the corral behind him. She'd obviously noticed that Donny and Cochise were being worked inside the pen. The smile dropped from her lips.

Donny must have spotted her. As Ethan glanced over his shoulder, the boy lifted his hand in a wave.

With him no longer maintaining a firm grip to control Cochise, the horse lowered his head and gave a solid buck, followed by a trio of hops. Donny came out of the saddle and was almost thrown over the horse's head. Luckily, he remembered to grab the horn, and a moment later he was back in command.

Hugh whipped the lunge line in the animal's direction, issuing harsh orders. Cochise settled immediately.

Ethan turned back to Cassie.

She looked pale as milk, her mouth slightly parted and a look of absolute terror in her eyes. As Ethan reached her, he saw a sickly tinge of green around her lips.

"Cassie? You all right?"

She looked at him. "What the hell is going on here?"

"What do you mean? We're giving lessons to Donny."

"To teach him what? How to get sent to the hospital?"

"You mean the bucking? He's doing great. Hasn't had a single toss."

"Yet," she snapped. Her voice sounded as brittle as glass.

Ethan reached out to rub his hand up and down her arm, feeling the tension within her. "Cass, relax. He's fine. If he takes a fall, the sand in there is soft, and he's wearing a helmet."

"Is that supposed to be reassuring? I don't care if he's wearing a full suit of armor. I've agreed that he can come over here to visit, but I don't want him doing *that*."

"In case you haven't noticed, it's not Donny doing it, it's Cochise. He has a few behavior problems, but nothing that can't be worked out of him."

"Then we'll sell him. I'm not having my son ride a dangerous horse."

"He's not dangerous."

"He nearly killed Ziggy." The anguish in her eyes scored Ethan's heart, but he managed to remain calm, practical.

"You know that was Ziggy's fault."

Shock had disappeared. He'd seen her angry before, but he'd never seen her eyes so cold or her face so hard. "Don't tell me what I know. Donny's not a rodeo cowboy. He's a twelve-year-old boy who just *thinks* he is. I'm sure he finds this all fun and games, but it's not."

"Of course it's not," Ethan replied. He felt his own temper start to take hold, and tried to remind himself that she was just a frightened mother. "Give him some credit. He's smart, and he's been working hard on Cochise's ground manners."

Her eyes were incredulous. "You mean you've been having him do this more than just today? Without clearing it with me?"

"I wasn't aware that I *had* to clear it with you," he said. Hearing the sarcasm in his voice, he tried to soften his tone. "Cassie, you're making too big a deal here. This is what I do. I've worked with dozens of riders with unruly mounts. I'm not going to let anything happen to Donny."

Her mouth twisted. "Like you didn't let anything happen to me?"

It took less than a moment for Ethan to feel the slice

of that cut. He stared at Cassie, trying to find the woman he'd made love to just the other night. There was no sign of her.

She slipped past him, heading for the corral. "Donny!" she yelled. "Stop that right now. Go home and wait for me."

Donny looked confused and annoyed. "But, Mom—"

"No argument. Go."

The boy responded with a sullen look, but he seemed to know that this was not the time to make a stand. He walked Cochise past Hugh as Quintin opened the gate for him. Neither man said a word. When Donny reached the field beside the corral, he urged the palomino into a trot and disappeared into the woods that led toward the Flying M.

Only then did Cassie turn to face Ethan again. Her eyes glittered. A feeling of dread began to spread within his chest. Still, her next words surprised him.

"I'm sorry about what I said just now. It wasn't fair."

"I understand that you're upset, but you're wrong about this," he told her, as calmly as his thudding heartbeat would allow.

She shook her head. "I don't care. I'm not going to let that horse hurt my son just so you can show him how cool you are."

His eyes narrowed. "You think that's what all this is about?"

"I don't know what to think. But I'm telling you this, Ethan. Stop working with Donny and Cochise. Immediately. We'll tell him you're his father, but if I find out he's over here, doing those kinds of things again, I'll tell my attorney to fight you for custody with everything we've got."

OF ALL THE MEXICAN restaurants in town, Donny liked Hot Tamales best, which was why Cassie had insisted that Josh take them there for dinner that evening. She supposed it was a foolish mother's trick to try to sweeten her son's disposition with a trip to one of his favorite places, but frankly, she was out of ideas for ways to patch things up with Donny. Since the argument they'd had this morning at breakfast over seeing Dr. Parker, and a second scene over his visits to Horse Sense, he'd hardly said two words to her.

Now they sat at a back table in Hot Tamales, waiting for a waitress to come, and listening to a mariachi trio play fun music that no one seemed to appreciate. Donny had his head down, as though enthralled by the menu. Josh shared a look with her that said it might be a long evening.

Earlier, she'd told him everything that had happened. Well, not everything. No need to mention that evening in the park with Ethan. She and Josh might be divorced, but somehow it just felt too awkward. In fact, *everything* felt off-kilter these days.

Since leaving Ethan at his hotel the other night, she had been going through the motions of an ordinary life. Oohing and aahing over the fish Josh and Donny had brought back from their camping trip, exercising in the Torture Chamber, scheduling feed deliveries, even checking the Internet for the best prices on a new truck. To the outside world she seemed perfectly normal, but on the inside she wasn't even on the same planet as everyone else.

She had been somewhere faraway, someplace new and wonderful…and dangerous. Because she had been with Ethan. And for as long as she could, she wanted to hold on to that wonderful part, without worrying about the rest.

Not that she was foolish enough to think her whole life could change because of a few hours of great sex. Not even earth-shatteringly great sex. She and Ethan still had a lot of issues to work out concerning Donny. There were bound to be differences of opinion ahead—just like the one today. And while she might be head-over-heels in love with him, she'd had no indication that he felt the same way. For him, it might be all about the sex.

While she'd been in his arms, she'd felt a connection too profound to be merely physical, a heady sense that everything was, at long last, right with her world. She'd been more than a little amazed, really, at just how right it had felt.

But did Ethan share that feeling? Was it possible that he, too, thought there was a chance for them to start over?

She'd had an opportunity to find out when she'd finally worked up the courage to drive over to see him this morning. She'd been so determined, so full of hope. Just the sight of him had made her breathing hitch.

But hope had shriveled when she'd spotted Donny in the corral and watched him be nearly unseated by Cochise. She was sure that her heart had stopped beating in that moment. He could have been trampled, or killed, and all on Ethan's watch. Was that how he intended to look after their son? How could he have such careless disregard for his own child?

Of course, thinking about it now, she realized that her reaction had been…a little over the top. As Ethan had said, working a horse and rider like that was what he did for a living. What he did best. She should have given that more consideration. She should have trusted him not to put their son in danger.

But the bottom line was she'd been too scared to do anything but lash out.

So…where did that leave her relationship with Ethan now? she wondered. Should she call him? Should she let it pass and pretend it hadn't happened? Should she show up at his hotel room dressed in the sexiest lingerie she could find? Oh, damn! She'd been out of circulation too long to know what to do.

Josh caught her attention with a tap on her arm. She looked up from the menu to see that a server had come to their table and was waiting patiently to take her order.

"I'll have the soft taco platter," Cassie said quickly. "Extra sour cream."

Josh chuckled. "All that studying the menu, just to end up ordering your usual."

She gave him a don't-mess-with-me look and handed her menu back to the waitress.

Even Josh seemed determined to annoy her tonight. When she'd told him about the argument she'd had with Ethan at Horse Sense, he hadn't immediately taken her side. Donny and Cochise had to learn to work together, he'd said. The fact that Ethan was willing to teach them was a good thing. Cassie had been so peeved by his attitude that she'd locked herself in the Torture Chamber and ridden an extra ten miles on her stationary bike.

"I'll take the beef burrito," Donny told the waitress.

Josh's eyebrow lifted. "I thought—"

He broke off as Cassie kicked him under the table. She knew he'd been ready to tease Donny about his lack of commitment to a vegetarian diet, but tonight wasn't the time for it. Donny was surly enough as it was.

Conversation around the table remained desultory and edgy, so it was good that no one seemed inclined to talk much.

Donny rose from the table. "I gotta go pee."

"You need to go to the restroom," Cassie corrected almost automatically.

"Whatever."

As soon as the boy was out of sight, she turned to Josh. "Do something. Make him talk. Make him be the sweet child I gave birth to."

Josh finished off the salsa-covered chip he was eating, then gave her a small smile. "Stop trying to control things, Cassandra. Have we ever been able to make him talk when he doesn't want to?" He wiped his mouth with his napkin. "And if we do, he's only going to say things you don't want to hear."

"I don't care. At least we might get to a point where we can actually have a discussion. But he's so angry with me right now he'd disagree if I said the sky was blue."

"He'll get over it. Why do you want to push him?"

"Because when he meets with Dr. Parker, I don't want him going in there with attitude, looking like he's got a bunch of problems. I want him to be open-minded. I don't want him stonewalling."

"Parker seems like the kind of guy who knows his stuff. He'll see through whatever crap Donny tries to pull."

She gave Josh a close look, realizing she was a little desperate for reassurance. "Do you really believe that?"

"I do. It's going to be all right. I'd be more concerned about Rafferty."

"Why do you say that?"

Josh made a face. "Well, we want Ethan's cooperation, right? I just hope we can still get it now that you've managed to piss him off completely."

"I was protecting Donny."

He looked around, as though seeing the restaurant for the first time. Probably just stalling. "Were you?" he asked at last. "Or were you just caught up in memories of your own accident?"

Cassie frowned at him. "I think you should leave analyzing to Dr. Parker."

"And I think you ought to acknowledge a truth when it's staring you in the face."

"What truth?"

"That the past still has a hold on you. You still have unresolved feelings for Rafferty, and they color everything you think, do or say."

She exhaled a deep breath. One thing about Josh, he didn't pull any punches. "I'm pathetically obvious, aren't I?"

"Well…" he said, looking at her affectionately. "I've known you a long time."

"Do you think Donny's noticed?"

"No. But sooner or later, if things get any more serious between you and Ethan, you'll have to tell him. We'll all have adjustments to make."

"I'm not sure how much more 'adjusting' he can take.

Or me, for that matter. I feel like my world's upside down as it is."

Josh toyed with his water glass for a long moment. He took a swallow, then set it down carefully. Without looking at her, he said, "I'm afraid I'm not going to make it any easier."

Confused by that comment, Cassie caught his eyes again. "What does that mean?"

"Believe it or not, I'm dating."

She stared. Whatever she had expected him to say, that certainly hadn't been it. "A *woman?*" she asked in an incredulous tone, then added quickly, "I mean, who?"

"Meredith Summerlin."

"Our Realtor? You're kidding."

"No. We went out on our first date last week."

"How did it go? What did you do?"

"It went fine. I took her to lunch."

"Where?"

"Pork Palace."

"A barbecue place! You don't take a woman to a barbecue place on your first date! It's too messy and unromantic."

Josh grinned at her. "Sorry, I missed the memo. She seemed to like it."

"Tell me everything."

"I will not. A gentleman doesn't kiss and tell."

Impatience had her cocking her chin at him. "You kissed her?"

"I'm not going to give you the details, Cassandra," he said with a laugh. Then he shook his head. "This whole thing is definitely too weird."

"What's weird about it?"

"Telling my wife about my date with another woman."

"Your *ex*-wife as of six months ago, so it's not the same. Besides, I still want you to be happy."

"Then let me just say that dating Meredith makes me happy."

"I'm glad," Cassie said with real pleasure. "Are you going to see her again?"

"I don't know. I want to. When I was camping with Donny, I had plenty of time to think. I realized that a lot of changes are coming our way."

"Because of Ethan."

Josh nodded. "Especially if Ethan becomes…more to you than just a man you share custody with. It's quite possible I'll end up getting left behind."

"I will never, *ever* let that happen."

He took her hand and squeezed it. "I know you won't if you can help it, but it may just…evolve. Which is why I think I need to start reinventing my life. But I don't want to do anything to confuse Donny needlessly."

"Confuse me about what?" Donny asked as he came around the corner of the table and sat down.

Cassie glanced at Josh, wondering how much the boy had heard.

Without the slightest hesitation, Josh said, "I don't want you to be confused about why we've made this appointment to see Dr. Parker. It isn't because we don't love you, or because you've done anything wrong."

Donny spent a long time realigning his silverware. When he looked up, his eyes were very dark, very intense, and his jaw was hard as a rock. "Did the shrink tell you to tell me that?"

Cassie understood bravado, but there were limits to

what she'd put up with. Besides, if she was too easy with Donny, he'd become more suspicious than ever. She gave him a hard gaze. "His *name* is Dr. Parker. And no, he didn't tell us to say that."

"I'm not stupid, you know," Donny said mysteriously. "I know a lot more that goes on than either of you think."

She didn't know what her son meant by that, and with a quick glance at Josh, she saw that he didn't, either. It rattled her a little, but there was no time to address it because the waitress had arrived with a trayful of dishes.

Donny helped the woman get the plates to the right person. Drawing a shaky breath, Cassie met Josh's eyes again. He offered her a smile of reassurance. There was no need for words. The appointment with Dr. Parker could be the start of something good. Or a complete disaster.

They both hoped for the best, but because they knew Donny, they would have to prepare themselves for the worst.

CHAPTER SIXTEEN

CURSING, ETHAN STOMPED into the campsite tent and would have slammed the door if it had had one. His headache had gotten worse, and after last night's drinking, his stomach was far from steady. He held his left hand up to the light, checking the damage.

The staple gun had barely imbedded one staple into the base of his palm. There was hardly any blood. It didn't even hurt much. Lucky for his father.

Today had all the signs of being a real barn burner. Nothing seemed to be going right, nothing, and Ethan was losing patience with Hugh, who seemed all thumbs this morning. Quintin usually ran interference between them, but he was in town, arranging deliveries and picking up a few things from the tack shop.

Ethan and Hugh had started off the day determined to finish up the cross-tie chutes they'd been erecting next to the corral, where problematic horses would be placed to allow access to them without the possibility of hurting themselves or a rider. Nothing too complicated. Pretty simple construction, really.

No such luck. First they had discovered that the wrong wood had been sent out from the lumberyard. Second, it hadn't been cut to specifications. It had been measured out longer than necessary, so they weren't at a standstill workwise, but Ethan had been forced to saw all morning just to get the pieces the right length.

Finally, Hugh had said he would man the staple gun while Ethan pounded nails, and like a fool, he had let him. When the pneumatic device got away from the older man, Ethan had just missed having his left hand fastened to a railing. Hugh had apologized, but the near accident hadn't sweetened Ethan's mood any.

Okay, he told himself. *Calm down. No real damage done.* He'd survived worse with only a few permanent scars. It wasn't as though his father had done it on purpose.

Besides, he knew a lot of his frustration today had nothing to do with Hugh. Yesterday's confrontation with Cassie had soured his attitude. Hell, it had done a lot more than that. It had pissed him off big-time. It had also made him realize that there were still plenty of obstacles ahead, still lots of work to do if they had any hope of having a relationship again.

Would they ever really be able to put the past behind them and start fresh? Sometimes it seemed so damned unlikely.

But what could he do? He was crazy about her, couldn't wait to see her again. They'd wasted years trying to move on, make new lives. But no more. He was done with settling for loneliness and isolation, keeping people at arm's length under the pretense of needing to concentrate on building a business. It was a lousy hand he'd dealt himself, and it was time he stopped playing it.

He wanted Donny in his life. And he wanted Cassie there as well.

The only problem was persuading her that it was right for all three of them to be together. As a family.

As he pulled the first-aid kit out from one of the duffel bags, he heard movement behind him. His father stood in the tent's opening.

"Well?" Hugh said. "Are you going to lose the hand?"

Ethan scowled over his shoulder.

"I said I was sorry," his father added. He sounded mulishly determined to downplay what had happened. "It was just a little staple. They use bigger ones when they have to sew you up in surgery."

Ethan found a pair of tweezers, then cotton balls and, finally, a bottle of hydrogen peroxide. He went past his father without a word. Outside, the light was better.

When Ethan plucked the staple out of his hand, his father examined the two holes it had left. "Doesn't look too bad," he said.

"Let me staple you and see how you like it."

"With all this fuss over a tiny puncture, I guess you'll never get your ears pierced."

Hugh's lips twitched, but his attempt at humor fell flat. "Do you want to talk?" he asked as Ethan wiped away the blood.

"No, I want to finish those chutes so I can honestly say we accomplished something today."

"I don't mean talk about stapling you," Hugh said. "I mean, do you want to talk about what happened yesterday between you and Cassie? I know it's got your hackles up. Quintin said you tied one on last night that would put even my drinking to shame."

"Quint talks too much."

"Listen here, son. You think life between a man and

a woman is a bed of roses just because they're in love? Never gonna happen. Tempers flare. You have differences of opinion. That's what keeps it interesting. What do you want? A Stepford wife?"

With a harshly exhaled breath, Ethan splashed peroxide over his hand, then shook it to remove the excess. He straightened to meet his father's eyes. "I'll tell you what I *don't* want. I don't want a lecture from a man who—" Cutting himself off, he recapped the bottle and tossed the peroxide into the first-aid kit. "I don't need advice on my love life. Let's tackle those chutes again. This time, *I'll* take the staple gun."

"Talking this out would be a lot better for you," Hugh stated. "You need a plan of action to win back Mrs. Wheeler."

"I don't need a plan of action to win back anyone. Cassie will come to me eventually, once she's thought things through. What I do need are employees who *do* what I tell them to."

"Fine!" Hugh said, throwing up his hands in surrender. He retrieved the staple gun from a camp chair. "Be as stubborn as your old man. No one can say I didn't try."

Father and son glared at each other for a few moments. Ethan was just about to swing around and head back to the chutes when they both heard hoofbeats coming fast. They turned to see Donny on Cochise, galloping out of the woods in their direction.

Horse and rider reached them in no time. A snorting Cochise slid to a halt as Donny jumped down from the saddle in one smooth movement, kicking up dirt and blades of grass.

"Pretty cool, huh?" the boy said. "Just like in the movies."

Hugh pretended to fan dust out of the air. "Good way to get yourself tossed."

Donny ignored the complaint. He grinned at Ethan. "Bet you didn't expect to see me so soon after Mom freaked out yesterday."

Ethan returned his son's smile, but when he looked in Donny's eyes, he got a different message entirely. Edgy. Desperate. Beseeching, and a little afraid. And his words, although pleasant enough, had a brittle, taut quality to them. Something was up.

"What are you dong here?" Ethan asked.

"Nothing. Can't a guy visit his friends?"

"Sure you can." He frowned. "But is something wrong?"

The boy shrugged. His gaze fell to his hands, which were threading Cochise's reins through his fingers over and over again.

"What's wrong?" Ethan repeated in the most fatherly tone he could muster.

His son's shoulders hunched. "I just had a fight with Mom and Dad," he admitted, then grimaced. "Number two hundred and sixty-two this week."

"Do you want to talk about it?" Hugh asked.

"Nothing to talk about, really. I got into a little trouble at school. Once they talk to the principal, I know they're going to make a big deal out of it. I'll probably be locked up for good. They just keep treating me like a little kid, no matter how I try to tell them that I'm not anymore."

Ethan felt his stomach twist. This was so far out of his realm of expertise it was laughable. But Donny had come here, to him. He had to say something reassuring, didn't he? Something wise and calming. He had to settle for something safe and pretty lame. "Parents have a hard time sometimes, accepting that their children are growing up."

That brought Donny's head up. Fast. "How would you know? I mean, you don't have any kids, do you?"

Ethan's heart banged into his throat. A real moment of truth, as they say. The lie was on his lips, but he found that he couldn't utter the words. His mouth felt like tinder, waiting for the flame. He exchanged a glance with his father. No help there. Ethan might as well have been shipwrecked, adrift on a raft.

His son wanted honesty. He had to give him that. At least, as much as he dared. "As a matter of fact, I do," he said simply. "We're just not together right now."

"Is he like you?"

"Two peas in a pod." Hugh tossed in the comment.

"Dad…" Ethan threw the older man a warning glance.

"Did you know Mom and Dad are making me see a shrink?" Donny asked.

"Yes."

"Did they tell you why?"

"I assume your mom thinks it will help you."

"Is it because I've made some pretty boneheaded moves lately? God, it's not like I'm turning into *The Omen* kid."

"You need to talk to them."

"Man," Donny grumbled, with a shake of his head. He was clearly dissatisfied with that answer. "Is *everyone* trying to keep me in the dark?" He glanced back up at Ethan. In a voice thickened by emotion and pouring scorn, he asked, "What does that mean, anyway? Help me how?"

"Your parents only want to do what's best. Talking it out with an expert might make you feel better. It might sort things out for you."

"What things?" Donny's eyes narrowed when Ethan said nothing to that. "I know you know something. Every time I walk into a room my folks stop talking. But I've heard stuff, and somehow, you're part of it. I just don't know what part."

"I can't help you with this, Donny. You'll have to ask your parents."

"Like that will do any good."

The boy looked dazed. He gave off waves of vulnerability. It didn't last long. No more than a moment or two. Then his features became pinched. "Okay, so don't tell me. Give me a lesson instead. Cochise can use the workout."

"Looks to me like you've already given him one," Hugh said.

Ethan shook his head. "We have work to do. I can't give you one today."

Thwarted again, the boy clenched his jaw. "You really don't want me around, do you?"

"Not this way. You're too worked up to have control. It would be pointless."

"No, it wouldn't."

"I said no," Ethan told him, fighting to keep his voice even. Donny had just about exhausted his patience. "Besides, your mom doesn't want you over here, putting Cochise through his paces. Remember?"

"I don't give a damn what my mom wants."

Frustration tightened in Ethan. What more could he

say to settle Donny down? What more *should* he say? Was he just supposed to tolerate this kind of outburst? There was a stubborn warrior's gleam in the boy's eyes, and nobody had given Ethan a playbook on how to handle this sort of thing.

Finally, he said in a quiet, stern voice, "Come back tomorrow. When you've had some time to rethink your behavior."

"I'm never coming back."

"That would be a shame, but it's your decision."

Donny's face went bloodred. "You're an asshole, you know that?"

Dead silence stretched out for a long moment. Ethan fought away his surprise by pretending not to have felt it. He hadn't been young for a long time, but he remembered that kids suffered a lot when they were confused and angry. He couldn't condone this fit of temper, though, no matter how sorry he felt for Donny.

He gave his son a disappointed shake of his head, then began gathering a few tools he'd need to finish work on the cross-tie chutes.

From the corner of his eye, he saw Donny jerk hard on Cochise's reins as he looped them into his hand, preparing to mount. The palomino tossed his head, startled at being mishandled.

Hugh made a disapproving sound. "Ease up, young one," he told the boy. "Don't take your temper out on your horse."

Donny swung up into the saddle. "Don't tell me what to do!" he shouted. "Teddy Delmar told me all about you trying to cheat his dad at cards. He says you're nothing but a used-up old wino looking for a handout."

Ethan swung around. "That's enough!" he said

sharply, unable to hang on to his own anger in spite of his best intentions. "That's your grandfather you're talking to!"

"I don't care—"

Donny halted.

For several measured heartbeats they just stared at one another. The kid was quick. His eyes widened and his mouth went slack with shock as he absorbed that news and put the pieces together. He scowled in disbelief.

Ethan moved toward his son. As though scorched by his proximity, Donny backed Cochise away.

Ethan had no idea how he could fix this, but he knew he had to try. "Donny—"

"I knew there was something going on," the boy said in a raspy voice, as though he'd just had the wind knocked out of him. "I knew it! I just didn't know what…" His head swung back and forth. "You can't be my dad. You're a liar."

"I'm sorry. We need to sit down and talk—"

Donny pulled hard on the reins, until Cochise came up on his hind legs. "Don't come near me! Leave me alone!"

He swung the horse around and kicked him into a gallop.

"Donny!" Ethan shouted, but the boy didn't look back and only increased Cochise's speed until they were running full-out. A moment later they disappeared into the woods.

Ethan muttered an obscenity.

"Think he'll head for home?" Hugh asked.

"He'll want answers."

Grabbing his cell phone off his belt, Ethan punched

in Cassie's number. He knew he had to get in touch with her right away, though he didn't relish telling her what he'd done. She'd probably never believe that it hadn't been intentional. But days of frustration and little sleep, combined with fruitlessly trying to make a surly preteen be sensible, had taken its toll on his judgment. He'd been—

Oh, hell. Forget the blame game for now. What's done is done. Just do your best to fix it.

The housekeeper at the Flying M answered, telling him that no one was home. As far as Mercedes knew, the mistress was out running errands. If he needed to talk to her, she had her cell phone.

Needed to talk to her? That was an understatement. He memorized the number that the woman gave him, but when he tried it, the call went unanswered. Not even voice mail kicked in.

He punched Redial again and again. Still no answer. Desperate to reach Cassie, Ethan jumped into his truck. To his surprise, Hugh slid into the passenger seat.

The older man gave him a hard look, as though daring Ethan to chase him off. "I figure whatever's coming, you can use someone to back you up."

Ethan did nothing more than nod. He would track Cassie down in person if he had to. Or maybe he'd be able to find Donny. Anything was better than sitting here waiting for all hell to break loose.

CASSIE SAT IN THE passenger seat of Josh's car, but when he pulled into the front driveway of River Bottom, she made no move to get out.

She was still too stunned.

The two of them had just returned from a meeting

with Abe Sheffield, the principal at Donny's school. Just walking into his office, Cassie had felt like a truant student. This was the second time they'd met with the man in two weeks. First, that stupid fight Donny had gotten into. Now this…this impossible-to-accept accusation.

"I still can't believe it," Cassie said, realizing that this was about the sixth time she'd said it.

Josh made no move to get out of the car, either. His hands still gripping the wheel, he shook his head. "Neither can I, but Sheffield says Donny confessed."

Principal Sheffield had informed them that less than a week ago, vandals had spray-painted one outside wall of the gym. They'd drawn some pretty crude, but graphic pictures of the school mascot, a black stallion named Rocky, in the midst of the romantic pursuit of a mare. All anatomically correct.

It didn't help that the drawings were accompanied by various comments regarding Principal Sheffield's lack of ability in that department. When she saw the graffiti, Cassie had been so taken aback she'd had to sit down.

Donny involved in *this?* The kid couldn't even draw a stick figure!

But an intense, three-day investigation had revealed the culprits—two older boys who had been in trouble at school most of their lives. One of them had immediately fingered Donny as the third accomplice, and when he'd been called to the principal's office, it hadn't taken him long to confess. Even then, Sheffield had told Josh and Cassie, Donny had been disrespectful, defiant and sullen.

"It had to be the others, putting him up to it," Cassie said, still sounding mystified. "Why would he do such a thing?"

"I don't know. But even if he was just along for the ride, that doesn't make him any less guilty."

She turned in her seat to catch Josh's eyes. "I know. I just feel so…undone."

"We'll have to punish him, of course."

"I agree. We need to do something in addition to what Sheffield wants." Besides suspending Donny for three days, the principal had suggested hours of community service for the school. "Maybe we should forbid him to ride Cochise for a month?"

"He'll be furious, but yes, I think it's appropriate."

"I just wish I knew why. This isn't like him. I'd blame Ethan, but since Donny doesn't know who he really is…"

There was silence in the car for a few long moments. Finally, Josh said, "I blame myself."

"What?" Cassie said in surprise. "Why?"

"I'm the one who rocked his world off its axis. If I'd never strayed… If I'd just learned to be happy with the way things were…"

Cassie leaned over to grab his arm and give it a shake. "Don't say that. A decade's a long time to work on a marriage that never had a very good chance to begin with. I know it was a tough decision to make because of Donny, but we did the right thing, getting divorced. No more pretending. No more feeling guilty. We both deserve to be happy, Josh." That won her a small smile, so she plunged ahead. "We'll get through this. Dr. Parker will help us. And once we tell Donny about Ethan…"

Josh sighed heavily. "God help us. Who knows how he'll react?"

"Dr. Parker will be there to help guide us," Cassie said. It occurred to her that she'd been telling herself that so often these days that it was beginning to sound like a mantra.

They both heard it at the same time. Galloping hooves. A horse running fast, full-out. Bright sunlight coming through the windshield made Cassie squint as she tried to find the source. Shading her eyes, she saw a horse and rider emerge from the trees that bordered River Bottom's front pasture.

She recognized the golden horse right away, and the boy hunched low on Cochise's back. "It's Donny!" she said, getting out of the car. "What's he doing here? I told him to stay home until I got back."

Josh was exiting the car, too. She heard him say, "He's riding too hard."

Cassie waved her arms. "Donny, slow down!" she shouted. "Donny!"

In an instant her pulse began to pound. It felt as though her heart might jump out of her chest. Even the best riders didn't run full-out on uneven ground like that. Donny knew better. What was he thinking?

She saw him cross the pasture, then navigate the hard-packed dirt road. Finally, he began to zigzag through the pines that led to the house.

"Stop!" she yelled at him.

But Donny didn't stop, and the trees, their dark limbs like grasping, hurtful demons, seemed determined to punish him for such foolishness. Josh and Cassie were already running toward him when Donny swung Cochise around one of the pines and miscalculated how much space he would need to clear it.

Cassie jerked to a halt and watched as, almost in slow motion, her son was raked out of the saddle by one of the low-hanging limbs. Like a circus tumbler, he flew off Cochise's back, hit the ground and lay still.

She couldn't scream.

She couldn't breathe.

All she could do was stand there, numb, as Josh ran past her.

CHAPTER SEVENTEEN

ETHAN HIT THE emergency-room doors at a run, his father only a few steps behind him.

"Sit down, Dad," he said, pointing to chairs lined against one wall. "I'll see what I can find out."

Hugh could do nothing more than nod. He was out of breath after their jog from the parking lot.

Not knowing what else to do, Ethan had driven up and down just about every street in Beaumont, hoping to spot Cassie's truck. Josh Wheeler hadn't answered his cell phone, either, and with both of them out of touch, Ethan had a bad feeling that went all the way to his toes.

When the housekeeper from the Flying M called to say that Cassie and Josh were on their way to the hospital with Donny, that feeling turned into terror as black and deep as an abandoned well.

"Is it serious?" he had asked.

"I don't know," the woman had told him, but her voice sounded shaky.

"Which hospital?"

"Saint Agnes."

And now here he was, at the same hospital they'd taken Cassie to all those years ago.

Being in the emergency room was like going back in time. With the exception of a few slight updates, everything looked as if it had been caught in a time warp.

The utilitarian furniture, the faded tiles, even the health advisement posters on the wall.

So many years ago Ethan had followed Cassie's stretcher into this room. His heart had been beating in a fast, blind panic, just the way it was now. His son was lying somewhere in this bleak corner of the hospital. Hurt. Helpless. And all because Ethan had lost his temper.

But how bad? How bad?

He strode to the reception desk, edging aside a middle-aged man who stood there filling out forms. He wanted to make eye contact with the woman in charge.

"Please," he said in his friendliest tone. "Can you help me? I'm looking for Donny Wheeler. Twelve years old. Just brought in a short while ago, I think."

"He's here," the receptionist confirmed, after consulting her computer for what seemed like an endless time. "He's in a trauma room right now. His parents are with him."

"Trauma?" How ominous that sounded. "What does that mean?"

"Sir, if you'd like to take a seat, I'm sure—"

"No, I don't want to take a seat. I need to find out what's happening."

"Sir—"

"Get someone," he told her, unwilling to be pushed aside. "Get someone right now. I need to know."

The woman's features were openly hostile now. He didn't care. He wasn't going to sit meekly, waiting for some crumb of information to drop into his lap. He'd done that once, and he wouldn't do it again.

A hand fell on his arm. He turned to find Cassie at his side.

"What are you doing here, Ethan?"

He pulled her away from the desk, toward the quietest corner he could find. He studied her face, searching for signs, *any* sign that would give him a clue about Donny's condition. All he saw was a mother who looked gray and hollow-eyed, filled with nothing but fear.

"How is he?" he asked.

"I don't know. The doctor's still checking him over."

"How did it happen?"

She seemed almost disoriented. She had to focus on him and blink once or twice, just to find words. "I was at Josh's place. Donny came flying in on Cochise. He got tossed when he tried to go under a tree limb."

Ethan raked a distracted hand through his hair. "Oh, God. I can't believe this."

"Why can't you?" she asked, tilting her head. Her eyes had the look of glass marbles shattered from within. "He came to before we got him here, and told us a little of what happened. You didn't think Donny would be upset when he found out who you were?"

"Cass, it wasn't the way you think."

"I'm sure you'll have all kinds of explanations for how it happened. I know he said terrible things, especially to your father. I can understand why you'd be angry, but how could you have told him? We had an agreement…" She bit her lip and glanced away as though to compose herself. When she turned back, she seemed more determined, calm. "Look, the only thing I care about right now is my son. I have to go back."

"I'll come with you."

"No," she said, placing a hand against his chest. "You've done enough harm."

Sudden anger kept him from flinching. "I'm his father, damn it. I have a right."

The look on her face chilled him. She was freezing him out.

"Don't do this, Cass. Don't shut me out. I let you and your father chase me off all those years ago, and we've both agreed it was a huge mistake. Let's not make another one, not when we're just beginning to find a way back."

"This isn't about you and me. It's about Donny. And I don't want you in there. He's in pain. He's upset. I don't want you making it worse. You dropped a bomb into his universe. Now let us try to clean up the mess."

Anger was suddenly a hot barb in his gut. Ethan had come a long way since he'd returned to Beaumont, and he wasn't about to surrender now. He loved this woman with all his heart. He loved his son. But the gloves had to come off. Certain truths needed to be told. "Why, Cass? So you can try to manipulate things the way you want? From the moment I came back you've been trying to control things, trying to push everyone into doing what you think is best."

She stiffened. "That's ridiculous."

"You can blame me for this, and I'll assume it for making a poor decision. But you can't let yourself off the hook. You've confused and frightened Donny more than I ever could. He needed to be treated with respect and honesty, and all you did was offer him whispers and mixed signals. It was bound to explode in all our faces."

"You don't know anything about twelve-year-old boys and what they need."

"I was that age once. I had a father who was an expert

at telling lies to himself and to his family. You may have had good intentions, and you may have wanted to protect Donny, but all you've done is make things much worse."

Cassie's mouth trembled, then firmed. "I'd really like you to leave."

"Don't worry, Cassie. Even *I* recognize a losing battle when I see it."

Furious, and feeling defeated, Ethan turned and stalked away, just as he had thirteen years ago.

CASSIE LEANED OVER Donny's hospital bed to gently stroke back a lock of hair that had fallen across his fore-head. He usually complained when she did something like that, claiming he was too old to be treated like a kid. But right now he was sound asleep, thanks to the sedative the doctor had prescribed, so she could baby him all she wanted.

His face in sleep always undid her, and she felt a lump of emotion in the back of her throat. With a featherlight touch, her fingers moved across one of the scrapes on his cheek. It looked so obscene, marring his pale flesh, but his condition could have been so much worse. A dislocated shoulder, a few cuts and bruises. The doctor had said he could go home tomorrow.

She heard Josh sigh from the other side of the bed. "We were lucky, Cassandra."

"I know," she said softly.

Though this was her son's first overnight hospital stay, there had been so many times in the past when Donny had scared the life out of them. Just the usual mischief and mayhem of a boy's world, but Cassie didn't think she'd ever get used to it.

Such a short time ago she'd been ready to read him the riot act over what he'd done at school. Punishment. Tough love. Somewhere down the line he'd have to atone for that behavior, but not right now. Right now, he was just her baby.

She glanced down at his arm, the one not encased in a sling. It was tanned and filling out with young muscle. His chin and jawline had lost the child's softness she had once loved to stroke. In the blink of an eye he'd be all grown up. Then what?

Donny had a rebellious need to embrace life. *Just like his father,* she thought.

From the moment she'd met Ethan, she'd been drawn to his unquenchable thirst for living, that intense desire to experience all life had to offer. He'd made her puny little chips of defiance toward her father seem insignificant. And when Ethan and she had finally agreed to elope, she'd felt euphoric at the thought of breaking free.

But now she knew how different it could seem from a parent's perspective. A child's connection to life was so fragile, like shards of venetian glass. So easily broken.

She remembered all the times she had watched Donny roughhouse with other boys to the point of injury, seen him take foolish chances, or lost him momentarily in the mall. She could remember the sudden drop of her heart when bad things had happened, and the relief she'd felt when all she had feared hadn't come true.

Was it so horrible to want to protect your child against such an uncertain world?

Holding on to Donny's hand, Cassie sank into the bedside chair. The adrenaline rush had evaporated.

She was so tired. It was nearly seven, and outside the hospital-room window, the lights of Beaumont were winking on for the evening.

"You must be starved," Josh said. "I'm going to check out the cafeteria. What would you like?"

"Nothing. I can't eat."

"Doesn't matter, I'm still bringing you back something."

He came around Donny's bed and reached her side. His hand squeezed her shoulder, then rubbed a few moments until some of the stiffness went away. In the old days, he'd been great at back rubs.

"It's going to be all right, Cassandra," he said in a low voice.

She gave him a half smile. "I'll hold you to that."

After Josh left the room, Cassie pressed her lips against her son's curled fingers. The scent was all Donny, and they were so warm against her ice-cold hand. Good circulation. That was a great sign, wasn't it? This time tomorrow he could be asleep in his own bed.

She thought about what lay ahead. The conversations they'd have to struggle through. The explanations she'd have to give him. She saw Donny frown in his sleep, as though concentrating on his dreams. Ethan had changed his young life with only a few words. Was that what he was dreaming of now?

She wanted to be angry with Ethan, but realized in that moment that she wasn't. Ever since she'd seen him in the emergency room, she'd been thinking about what he'd said. How she tried to control things, how she tried to manipulate the situation to her liking. Just like her father.

But she could see that delaying the inevitable had

only made it worse. The basic fact was that Donny was Ethan's son, and there was no sense hiding it, or trying to make it go away, or manage it. It just...*was*.

Tomorrow she would find Ethan, tell him that he'd been right. She hadn't handled this sensibly at all. Even though the cat was out of the bag, it could still work out. They could find a way, if he would just give her a chance.

Just how angry had he been when he'd left the hospital? Angry enough to make things difficult? Surely not. He seemed to genuinely care about Donny. He might hate her, but he wouldn't hurt his son.

Did he hate her? Was there any hope for them? Unlikely. The bright promise of their renewed relationship seemed all but dead if she looked at it realistically. But she didn't want to look at it realistically. She wanted to hang on to the foolish belief that they could still have a relationship. She was in love with Ethan. It was that simple.

Cassie shivered. The room was cold. If she intended to spend the night in the chair, she'd need a blanket. With a last glance at Donny, who was snoring softly, she rose and headed for the nurses' station.

The hospital corridor was quiet, filled only with the hum of machinery and a soft murmur of voices coming from the central nursing hub. The lighting had been dimmed, no doubt in the hope that visitors would leave soon so patients could settle down.

As she reached the nurses' desk, she glanced toward the waiting room on that floor. One person was seated there, hunched over, hands dangling between his legs.

Ethan.

Hardly daring to believe that he was more than a

mirage, Cassie walked slowly across the distance that separated them. Ethan must have heard her approach. He looked up and stood quickly.

"Is he all right?" he asked in almost a whisper.

There were lines etched around his mouth, shadows under his eyes. That lazy glint of supreme self-confidence was gone, replaced by a world-weary fear. He looked, she realized, the way Donny had when he'd finally returned to consciousness. He looked lost.

"He's going to be fine," she told him, then gave him the doctor's prognosis. "He's sleeping now."

The relief in Ethan's face could have powered a city, it was so bright. "Thank God for that."

She was still having a hard time accepting that he'd stayed. All these hours, he'd been right here. "You didn't leave."

"I was going to," he said. "It would have been so easy to walk out, but I couldn't. I won't. I'm Donny's father, Cass, whether you like it or not. I can't help that it's not convenient or comfortable or simple. I'm not trying to hurt anyone, especially our son. But there has to be a way we can make this work."

She nodded, beginning to feel hopeful again. "Lots of parents share custody."

"I don't want to share custody."

Ice slid through her veins. "Then what do you want, Ethan?"

He took her arms in his hands, his eyes meeting hers. "I want Donny in my life full-time, and I want you there beside him. Marry me, Cassie. Let's make it a package deal."

Her breath caught. She blinked, then stared at him, certain she had somehow made up this entire scenario in her mind. If she waited long enough, this would all disappear and she'd find herself back in Donny's room.

"Say something, damn it," Ethan said. "It's taken me hours to get up the courage to ask."

"Marry you? We're not talking about ordering a Happy Meal here. Marriage can't be taken that lightly. I've already made that mistake once. It should be a lifetime commitment."

"A lifetime ago it *was* a commitment. One we both made. You agreed to marry me then. You didn't even have to think twice about it. You said yes before I could get all the words out."

"We were very young. We were—"

"In love. And nothing's changed for me. I'm in love with you, Cassie, and always will be."

"Ethan…"

His features were suddenly solemn. "I know we're going to have a heck of a time trying to make all this right. But together, I think we can do it, if you'll just forgive me. Give me a real chance. Say you love me. It's not too late for us," he said with a slight note of desperation. "Just take that leap of faith you were going to take thirteen years ago."

Heat began to spread through her, warming all the cold, lonely places she'd ignored for so long. She felt panicked, trembling, but most of all…thrilled.

"Yes," she said huskily. "I love you, and I always have. I think in some way, all these years, I've been waiting for you to come back to me."

He pulled her close. A fluttering sensation spread out from her abdomen as he cupped her head in his hands. "I'm sorry it took so long. I should never have left."

He kissed her, slowly and gently, right there in the

waiting room. She felt his strength, his certainty flowing through her. When he pulled his mouth away from hers, her legs were so rubbery she could hardly stand. All she could do was press against him, letting her forehead rest against his shoulder.

She was so lucky to have this second chance. It left her filled with amazement that, against all odds, this had been given to her. It seared the breath in her chest to think how close she had come to losing him again.

Her head moved back and forth against his collarbone. "I'm so sorry, Ethan…"

He ran his hand down the back of her neck. "Sorry for what, sweetheart?"

"Sorry that I drove you away that night in the hospital. I should have been braver, more willing to believe that things could turn out all right. I should have been more like you."

He leaned away so he could find her eyes. "No," he said with a broad smile. "I fell in love with the woman you were then. The woman you still are."

"But it's true what you said earlier. I do try to control things. My motives seemed very clear to me at first, but somewhere along the line they got muddled. I thought I knew what was best for all of us. Instead, I ruined everything."

"You didn't. We made a beautiful son together. And we can have so much more. You'll see."

The confidence she saw in Ethan's face gave her courage. She wanted nothing in the world but to go on like this, to be in his arms. But there were still issues that had to be addressed, and very soon. Although she didn't let go of him, she pulled away so they could talk.

"When Donny wakes up, he's going to have a million

questions." She squeezed Ethan's hand. "Am I a complete coward to admit that I'm scared to death?"

He gave her one of his heart-stopping smiles. "Me, too," he admitted in a hoarse whisper. "I'd rather break a dozen broncs than ever hurt that kid." He lifted her hand, touching his lips to her palm. She shivered with desire. "But we'll do all right," he promised.

She could hardly draw breath. She was lost. Hopelessly. Irrevocably. In love. "How…how can you be so sure?" she gasped, as his lips found the pulse at her wrist.

"Because this time, no one's running away. This time we'll find the answers we need. Together."

CHAPTER EIGHTEEN

By Donny's birthday in October, Cassie had begun to have real hope.

She stood in the kitchen at the Flying M, scrutinizing the round layers of chocolate cake she'd pulled out of the oven just moments ago. They looked a bit lopsided. She'd have to prop up the cake on one side with a little icing, but it would do. She set them on the wire racks to cool.

This evening would actually be Donny's second celebration. The day before, on his real birthday, he and his friends had been driven out to Bayou Ridge, where a deserted ranch had been turned into a paintball park. She hadn't liked the idea, but she'd been outvoted. She'd stayed in the truck and tried to read while Ethan, Josh, Quintin and even Hugh accompanied the eight boys and made sure no one ended up hurt.

Not her idea of a great birthday party, but one her son had asked for, and had been thrilled to share with his buddies.

Tonight, however, the adults in his life were coming over, and Cassie intended to stick to the traditional party theme. Cake, ice cream and gifts. Corny and low-tech, perhaps, but so what? Donny didn't mind—it only meant more presents for him—and it made her happy.

To be perfectly honest, being happy wasn't an unusual

state for Cassie these days, even though she and Ethan
had not married yet.

In the spring, when it had been so touch and go, she'd
been too leery of upsetting Donny with a wedding, and
she'd been relieved when Ethan had suggested they wait.
For now, it was enough for Cassie to have him back in
her life.

Donny had been shocked when he'd learned more of
the truth about his parentage. It was obvious that he liked
Ethan—he'd apologized for his behavior half a dozen
times—but he'd had a hard time coming to terms with
the news. Weekly visits with Dr. Parker had helped a
lot. Cassie had grown cautiously optimistic, even though
there were tears and tempers and mood swings to deal
with—especially when Donny had lost Cochise for a
month as punishment for his part in the gym vandal-
ism. But thankfully, they'd gotten through the rest of the
school year without further incident.

One tough hurdle they'd dreaded was the summer
vacation trip Josh, Cassie and Donny usually took with
the Stanleys. The adults agreed that it was impossible to
make it work. But surprisingly, when they'd told Donny,
he'd been fairly resigned to the news. After sulking for
two days, he seemed to accept the decision.

Cassie knew that she and Ethan owed Josh a debt they
could never repay. He'd been pivotal in making all this
easier for everyone.

She had thought he would be furious with Ethan for
telling Donny the truth, but that night in the hospital,
he'd run into Hugh Rafferty in the cafeteria. Ethan's
father had told Josh everything that had happened at
Horse Sense, including how Donny's disrespectful actions had caused Ethan to snap. The knowledge had

softened Josh's anger a bit, so that while her son slept, the three of them were able to put aside their differences and formulate a plan of action.

Since then, Josh had tried to step back and allow Ethan to take the lead. Cassie knew it couldn't have been easy for him, but he seemed determined to make a new life for himself. Maybe the fact that he was still seeing Meredith Summerlin had something to do with it. Her bubbling, happy-go-lucky personality was contagious, and Cassie had witnessed a change in Josh. A good one. Just what he needed.

As for Ethan… He had been amazing. Patient with Donny no matter what. He never pushed. He never lectured. He let the relationship evolve at its own pace. He simply stood by, ready to listen, ready to counsel if asked. Ready to be a father.

He'd told her once that he didn't know how to be a parent, but it turned out he was wrong. He was a natural at it.

Now, with the leaves turning russet and gold, Cassie wanted to believe she saw little changes in their son. A willingness to accept Ethan and Hugh as part of his family. Fewer challenges of authority and less "acting out." His sense of security had not been damaged. His trust was still there. She knew better than to expect a radical change overnight, but they were making progress.

Glancing at the clock, Cassie washed her hands and left the kitchen, heading for the horse barn. Ethan still lived at one of the cabins built at Horse Sense, but he'd come over early at Donny's request. Cochise had started to limp a little.

She found the man she loved in the tack room,

whipping up a gooey black potion for the horse's hooves. It reminded her of the night long ago when she'd slipped out of her bedroom to join Ethan, intent on eloping.

As she had back then, she moved quietly forward and brought her hands around to his eyes. "Guess who?" she said. "And if you say any name but mine, the wedding's off."

He turned and grabbed her closer, grinning. "Kind of hard to call off the wedding when the date hasn't even been set yet."

"One day. Soon, I hope."

"How about Christmas?" Ethan asked. Then he buried his face in her neck to plant a series of kisses against her flesh. A ripple of desire shot through her, so strong that a moan escaped her lips.

"Wonderful," she told him, and she wasn't sure whether she meant his idea or his touch. Maybe both.

His arms came around her possessively, but he pulled back enough that he could meet her eyes. "Seriously?"

"Why not? If things keep—"

He cut her off with more kisses, the kind that made her wonder how long her heart could pound at this rate. She sighed in genuine disappointment when he stopped and pressed his forehead against hers.

"I love you," he said softly.

"I love you, too," she told him. "I've been given my second chance at happiness, and I'm not going to ever let it get away."

"Ethan!" They heard Donny calling. "Where are you?"

Ethan turned Cassie loose with a regretful smile. "In the tack room!"

Donny appeared in the doorway moments later. She

and Ethan were careful not to be too demonstrative in front of him, but she knew their son was perfectly aware that they were in love. Just last week, Donny had cornered her in the Torture Chamber and asked her if she and Ethan were going to get married.

After stumbling through a lot of words that made no sense at all, she had settled on a very weak, "Maybe someday."

Donny had just shaken his head and laughed. Before he'd trooped out of the room, he'd told her, "Boy, you should see your face. If I look like that when I'm guilty, no wonder I get in so much trouble."

Ethan picked up the jar of salve he'd mixed for Cochise. He held it out for Donny to smell.

"Man, that stinks. What are you going to do with it?"

"I think Cochise has picked up a pebble and it's trying to work its way out the top of his hoof. This ought to draw it out more quickly. Shall we give it a try?"

Donny nodded.

Cassie followed them out of the tack room. Cochise was cross-tied in the barn corridor. He stood patiently, his ground manners greatly improved in the past few months Ethan had been working with him. It wasn't completely dark yet, and the shadows made the warm pool of barn light seem cozy and intimate.

She watched as Ethan passed the jar and a small brush to Donny, then lifted one of Cochise's front hooves.

"I'll hold and you paint," he told their son. "Okay?"

Cassie knew they were hardly aware of her presence now. Just two guys, caught up in working together. "Don't be too long," she said. "Everyone should be here soon."

Again Donny nodded. So did Ethan.

She turned to leave them.

"Easy, boy," she heard Ethan croon to Cochise. "Easy."

"Hold on to him, Dad," Donny said. "I can do this."

Cassie turned back. She exchanged a glance with Ethan. It didn't happen all that often, but it thrilled her every time Donny called him Dad. But even more, she knew how much it affected Ethan.

They tried not to make a big deal of it, but when she headed toward the house, she couldn't help smiling. She carried the picture in her head all the way back—the two most important men in her life. Connecting. Bonding. How could she be anything but happy?

CAPPING THE CONTAINER of salve, Ethan turned to give Cochise one more look. The horse stood calmly munching hay, but all four hooves were pitch-black, coated with a healthy dose of medicine geared to draw out any foreign object wedged there.

"Will I be able to ride him tomorrow?" Donny asked.

"Sorry," Ethan replied. "He needs to stay on soft grass for a couple of days with no weight. No hooves, no horse, as my father says."

"Is Grampa Hugh coming tonight?"

"Yep," Ethan replied. "That all right with you?"

"Sure. Why wouldn't it be?"

Ethan had to admit he was pleased with his son's response. One of the unexpected surprises of the past few months was how close Donny and his grandfather had become. At first, given his father's past, Ethan wasn't sure whether that was a good idea or not, but they seemed to have formed a solid bond of friendship after Donny had apologized for the disrespect he'd previously shown.

So far, Hugh was happy to continue working for Horse Sense and sharing a cabin with Quint. Now that the clinic was up and running—starting slow, but showing definite signs of growing—Ethan even occasionally let Hugh help out with the cops and their mounts. His father seemed content.

As for their personal relationship, it was coming along. Ethan figured if Cassie could give Hugh a chance to be a real grandfather to Donny, why couldn't he?

He glanced at his watch. Still a little time before Cassie might come back looking for them.

"Do I really have to wear a tie tonight?" Donny asked. They had returned to the tack room and were putting things away while the salve dried on Cochise's hooves.

"Afraid so, pal. I've brought one, too. Your mom wants pictures, and I guess she thinks a tie will make us look respectable."

"Can't you talk her out of it? She listens to you."

Ethan laughed. "Your mother's a hard woman to convince."

"Is that why you two aren't married yet? Because you can't get Mom to say yes?"

Ethan stopped in his tracks, turning to find his son's eyes in the poor light. His heart skipped a beat as he wondered what to say. Donny seemed to be waiting for his answer with barely disguised eagerness. All the more reason to stick to the truth, Ethan figured.

"I love your mother, and I want to marry her," he

admitted softly. "But we've agreed to wait until the time is right."

"So when is that?"

"I don't know. I guess when you feel all right with it."

Donny chewed the inside of his cheek for a moment or two. Then he cocked a questioning glance upward. "If you two get married, does that mean I won't get to see my other dad anymore?"

"That will never happen. He loves you as much as I do, and I know how you feel about him."

The boy's chin jutted slightly. "Dr. Parker says it's okay to feel the way I do."

It might make things a little more difficult, it might mean that the family dynamic would change more slowly, but there was no way Ethan was going to chase Josh out of Donny's life.

"It is, Donny. It's perfectly fine." He grinned. "Besides, with a kid like you, I can use all the advice I can get from Josh. Two heads being better than one, you know?"

The boy laughed at that, then frowned. "But I don't want to hurt Mom, either. Or you…"

"Don't worry about your mom and me. We're together, and we can wait until you're good with it."

"I kinda feel good about it now."

Ethan's heart banged in his throat. "Really?"

"Yeah, really," his son replied. "I keep telling everyone I'm not a little kid anymore. I want Mom to be happy, and she's so happy around you it's embarrassing. So if it can't be my old dad who makes her feel that way, then I think it ought to be my new dad." He scrunched his nose. "Although I guess that, technically, *you're* my old dad, aren't you? It's confusing, but you know what I mean."

"I get the idea. Maybe sometime soon you can help me figure out where and when to pop the question."

"I'm not so good with that kind of mushy stuff," Donny complained. "But I'll make a deal with you."

Ethan eyed his son with mock suspicion. "What kind of deal?"

"I'll help you with Mom, if you convince her I don't need to wear a tie tonight."

"Consider it done," Ethan said quickly, and stuck out his hand.

They sealed the bargain and were walking back through the barn when they heard a car door slam. The sound of a woman's high giggle followed a moment later. Meredith, no doubt. With Josh.

Donny loped away to meet them. As Ethan reached the entrance of the barn, he saw Josh greet the boy effusively, laughing and teasing. Meredith was already hurrying up the front steps, where Cassie waited like an accomplished hostess, outlined by the light from the front windows.

When Cassie caught sight of him coming through the night shadows, he imagined her smile grew wider.

For a tiny second, Ethan thought about all the years that had led to this, all the wrong choices they'd both made, the anger and hurt two people could cause one another. But there were things that had been done right, too. The gift of a son. Maybe another someday. Or a little girl who would have her mother's red hair and loving spirit.

He had never dared to hope that his life could be like

that, but he was ready for it. Impatient even. He took the stairs two at a time, eager to reach Cassie's side. Eager to be absorbed into the strange, wonderful mix of people he now considered his family.

* * * * *

HARLEQUIN® *Super Romance*®

COMING NEXT MONTH

Available October 12, 2010

#1662 THE GOOD PROVIDER
Spotlight on Sentinel Pass
Debra Salonen

#1663 THE SCANDAL AND CARTER O'NEILL
The Notorious O'Neills
Molly O'Keefe

#1664 ADOPTED PARENTS
Suddenly a Parent
Candy Halliday

#1665 CALLING THE SHOTS
You, Me & the Kids
Ellen Hartman

#1666 THAT RUNAWAY SUMMER
Return to Indigo Springs
Darlene Gardner

#1667 DANCE WITH THE DOCTOR
Single Father
Cindi Myers

LARGER-PRINT BOOKS!
GET 2 FREE LARGER-PRINT NOVELS PLUS
2 FREE GIFTS!

HARLEQUIN®

Super Romance®

Exciting, emotional, unexpected!

YES! Please send me 2 FREE LARGER-PRINT Harlequin® Superromance® novels and my 2 FREE gifts (gifts are worth about $10). After receiving them, if I don't wish to receive any more books, I can return the shipping statement marked "cancel." If I don't cancel, I will receive 6 brand-new novels every month and be billed just $5.44 per book in the U.S. or $5.99 per book in Canada. That's a saving of at least 13% off the cover price! It's quite a bargain! Shipping and handling is just 50¢ per book.* I understand that accepting the 2 free books and gifts places me under no obligation to buy anything. I can always return a shipment and cancel at any time. Even if I never buy another book from Harlequin, the two free books and gifts are mine to keep forever.

139/339 HDN E5PS

Name _____ (PLEASE PRINT) _____

Address _____ Apt. #

City _____ State/Prov. _____ Zip/Postal Code

Signature (if under 18, a parent or guardian must sign)

Mail to the **Harlequin Reader Service:**
IN U.S.A.: P.O. Box 1867, Buffalo, NY 14240-1867
IN CANADA: P.O. Box 609, Fort Erie, Ontario L2A 5X3

Not valid for current subscribers to Harlequin Superromance Larger-Print books.

Are you a current subscriber to Harlequin Superromance books
and want to receive the larger-print edition?
Call 1-800-873-8635 today!

* Terms and prices subject to change without notice. Prices do not include applicable taxes. N.Y. residents add applicable sales tax. Canadian residents will be charged applicable provincial taxes and GST. Offer not valid in Quebec. This offer is limited to one order per household. All orders subject to approval. Credit or debit balances in a customer's account(s) may be offset by any other outstanding balance owed by or to the customer. Please allow 4 to 6 weeks for delivery. Offer available while quantities last.

Your Privacy: Harlequin Books is committed to protecting your privacy. Our Privacy Policy is available online at www.eHarlequin.com or upon request from the Reader Service. From time to time we make our lists of customers available to reputable third parties who may have a product or service of interest to you. If you would prefer we not share your name and address, please check here. ☐

Help us get it right—We strive for accurate, respectful and relevant communications. To clarify or modify your communication preferences, visit us at www.ReaderService.com/consumerschoice.

HSRLP10R

Love Inspired
HISTORICAL

INSPIRATIONAL HISTORICAL ROMANCE

Fan favorite

VICTORIA BYLIN

takes you back in time to the Wyoming frontier
where life, love and faith were all tested.

Wyoming Lawman

He sought truth and justice—
and found a family at the same time.

Available October wherever you buy books.

www.SteepleHill.com

Steeple
Hill®